MORGAN'S SQUAW

Morgan knew Lattimer was a whisker away from being killed. "Go easy, Lattimer," he said. "It's me you've been pushing."

Lattimer talked without looking at him. "I'll get back to you. Right now I got to deal with this snot nose. Let's have the gun, kid. Hand it over and I won't hurt you."

Morgan did the only thing he could do to save Lattimer's life. He hit him as hard as he could, not in the jaw, which was like a rock, but in the gut. Lattimer just grunted and swung around to give Morgan all his attention, crowding in with the two men behind him.

The kid's gun came out like a flash and he said, "You two keep out of it. Three against one ain't fair."

BUCKSKIN #42

MORGAN'S SQUAW

KIT DALTON

LEISURE BOOKS NEW YORK CITY

A LEISURE BOOK®

September 2006

Published by

Dorchester Publishing Co., Inc.
200 Madison Avenue
New York, NY 10016

ISBN 0-8439-3821-8

Visit us on the web at www.dorchesterpub.com.

Chapter One

Morgan had the bucket jammed down over Young Ticknor's head and was beating on it with both fists trying to exterminate the stupid son of a bitch. Young Ticknor was crying for mercy and Sid Sefton, the outfit's top hand, was trying to get Morgan to stop because Gen. Howard's buckboard had just driven into the front yard. Morgan wasn't aware of that because he was too busy trying to hammer Young Ticknor into the ground. Hissing like a just-pulled-in locomotive, Sid was grabbing at Morgan, saying, "Gen. Howard is right behind you, looking at your bad behavior. Come on now. Stop it!"

Morgan didn't want to let up. Young Ticknor deserved no less than death for spilling a bucket of creosote on his new San Antonio boots. And if not death, then at least a few hours staked out on an anthill. Morgan didn't want to stop—Sid could be trying to pull a fast one—but he did. When he turned his head there was his old friend, Gen. Oliver Howard, looking at him with disapproval from the seat of the buckboard.

The general, known far and wide as Bible-reading Howard, had lost his right arm in the Civil War. Now he was in his sixties, retired and looking old. A traveling rug was draped over the shoulders of his wool greatcoat. It was late May in Idaho, but the wind was cold. Morgan hadn't seen Gen. Howard for ten years.

Beside the general on the box was his driver, an ex-New York thug and Fighting 69th sergeant named Shandy Gibbons, a burly pug-faced Irishman with mean blue eyes. In his youth Gibbons had worked as a teamster when he wasn't running wild with the Bowery gangs. He had started driving for the general after the old boy lost his arm, and he was still at it more than 20 years later. Gibbons never drove the general anywhere without having a ten-gauge Greener shotgun and a .50-caliber Sharps rifle close at hand. Dangerous weapons for a dangerous man.

Morgan knew him from the Nez Perce War of ten years before. Anybody who wanted to get at the general had to go through this formidable ruffian. He didn't like Morgan, and it still showed.

"Be right with you, General," Morgan said, taking the bucket off Young Ticknor's head. "Gosh Almighty, boy, you ought to be more careful with that creosote." Morgan had other words in mind, but Gen. Howard didn't like bad language. "Creosote's supposed to go on the raw wood, not on my new boots."

Morgan's new boots were soaked inside and out with the yellow, oily wood preservative. Hard-earned money had paid for those boots and for an instant he wanted to kill Young Ticknor all over again. But he didn't.

Gen. Howard was climbing down, saying in his mild voice, "All is vanity, Morgan, fancy boots and everything else."

Morgan knew better than to try to help the old man. So did Gibbons. One armed or not, the general liked to do

2

for himself. But Morgan could see the years were telling on him, and it wasn't just the sunken cheeks or the white in his beard.

They shook hands. "Say hello to your old friend Shandy Gibbons," the general said.

Morgan nodded. "Good to see you again." That would have to do.

"Likewise," Gibbons said, looking at the horses in the corral. His mouth twitched as if he found something amusing.

Morgan felt like putting the Irishman head-down in the outhouse, but instead he said, "Light down and have something to eat."

"We et on the road." No word of thanks from this truculent bastard. "I'll just grain and water the horse, wait for the general." Gibbons hesitated. "I wouldn't mind a bottle of beer, if you have it."

"Bitsy will fetch it for you."

"Bitsy, eh?" Another smirk.

What in hell did he want, Morgan thought. Then he got it, what else? Gibbons thought Bitsy was a woman, not a tiny old Chinese cook.

"One bottle, Shandy," the general said, as down on alcohol as he was on swearing. He turned to Morgan. "I'd like to make this a real visit, but we have to be moving along. There's a good way to go before nightfall."

The men were waiting to be introduced to the famous old soldier, and they were shy as they stepped up to shake his hand. To most men in Idaho he would always be the hero of the Nez Perce War of '77. Young Ticknor, his hair and face oily with creosote, was hanging back, thinking it might be a good idea to stay clear of Morgan. Finally, he came forward like a bad dog expecting to be whipped.

"Looks like I got here just in time," the general said, making a point of shaking his hand. Young Ticknor's

3

handshake left the general's hand smeared with creosote. Morgan could have kicked him in the nuts. All the general did was say, "You're not related to the Ticknors of Boston, by any chance?"

"Not that I know of, sir," Young Ticknor said.

Morgan doubted that the kid even knew where Boston was. Odd as hell though, he wasn't as dumb as he looked when he was doing dumb things. Like spilling creosote on brand new boots. Like falling off the bunkhouse roof when Sid sent him up to look at a leak in the chimney. Like plenty Morgan could think of. Seemed as if he had two left feet. He couldn't do the simplest chore without making a mess of it. All he was good at was shooting guns, especially handguns, his only interest. The kid was crazy about guns, spent a good part of his wages on ammunition. On Sundays he practiced his draw and shot at targets in the woods. Once they were walking through some brush and he shot the head off a rattler that reared up in front of them. A lightning draw, a single shot, and the rattler was dead.

Sometimes he made Morgan uneasy, wondering what he was going to do next.

Going into the house the general said, "I guess you're wondering what I'm doing here. I didn't want to say anything in front of the men."

"The men are all right," Morgan said.

"I'm sure they are, but this is between you and me. You were a good scout, Morgan, best I ever had. Point is, I know you and I don't know them."

It was chilly in the house and Morgan put a match to the ready-stacked wood. The kindling caught and the seasoned cut-wood started to burn. Gen. Howard eased himself into a homemade leather armchair and stretched out his skinny legs, sighing with contentment. "You have a nice place here," he said, looking around the big main room with its wide-planked floor and huge stone fireplace.

"Always said you wanted a good horse ranch of your own. Looks like you finally got it."

"It's coming along," Morgan said, thinking how hard it had been to build up Spade Bit. In the years since the Nez Perce War they had exchanged very occasional letters without saying much of anything. The general wasn't much of a letter writer, and neither was he. Never once had Morgan mentioned the two or three streaks of bad luck that had come his way. You didn't whine like that to an old friend.

"You sure you don't want something to eat? A cup of coffee?" Morgan asked.

"No coffee, thanks. You know I don't hold with stimulants of any kind. But a glass of buttermilk would be good. A sure cure for high blood pressure, did you know that? Healthiest drink in the world."

The general had earned the right to be any kind of crank he wanted to be. Morgan yelled for Bitsy, the Chinaman, to bring buttermilk and after that to take a bottle of beer out to the general's driver. Gen. Howard fished a thick cigar from his vest pocket and bit off the end. When he got the buttermilk he sipped it with obvious enjoyment.

"Nice and thick—delicious," he said. The fire was warming the room.

Morgan never could understand why anybody in his right mind would want to drink the awful stuff. It wasn't as bad as horsepiss, which had saved his life one time in the desert, but it ran it a close second.

"Are you still as fond of beer as you used to be?" the general asked between swallows. He finished the buttermilk and lit the cigar.

"No, not as fond as I used to be," Morgan lied, hoping to ward off a lecture on the evils of beer.

The general puffed heartily on his cigar. "Glad to hear it. Granted it isn't as bad as whiskey, but it's bad enough. An addiction like any other."

Morgan smiled. "They say smoking is just as bad."

"Nonsense! Do you think I'd smoke if it was bad for me? The truth is, smoking is good for you. It calms the mind, it's an aid to reflection and clear thinking, not to mention what it does for the digestion."

Morgan wondered how long the general was going to go on like this. Maybe age was really getting to him. But he knew he was wrong about that when the general suddenly got right down to business.

"Of course you know who Cedric Halliday is. They call him Drick for short."

"It's better than Seedy," Morgan said.

The general wasn't much for jokes. "He smells no better whatever they call him. Do you know him?"

Morgan nodded. "I know of him. Who doesn't? Mines, ranching, lumber, fruitlands, a bank, newspapers, a narrow-gauge railroad, a string of trading posts started by his father. One of the richest men in Idaho, maybe the richest, or so they say. You want me to go on?"

The general nodded and Morgan continued, "Lately he's been going on about the Indian menace. But he's always been going on about the Indian menace. His newspapers have."

"Not like now," the general said. "Halliday is the reason I'm back here after so many years. All the way from Washington." Gen. Howard sighed. "Halliday, believe it or not, wants to forcibly remove all the Indian tribes from Idaho. Nez Perce, Bannacks, Shoshones, Lemhis, Sheepeaters—one way or another he wants them gone, rounded up and marched away under heavy guard. 'They have no place here. They stand in the way of civilization,' he says."

"I always heard he had a screw loose," Morgan responded.

"On the subject of Indians he does. Otherwise he seems sane enough. Of course, money is at the root of it, money and power, personal and political power. Idaho will be a state in a few years and my guess—hardly a guess—is that Halliday wants to be governor or the first U.S. senator from Idaho. I may be wrong about that: making the puppets dance is more his line. Be that as it may, he seems to think this so-called Indian problem will get him what he wants. Yes, yes, I know there hasn't been any Indian trouble for ten years, but Halliday doesn't see it that way.''

"Looks like he'd like to start an Indian war.''

"Maybe a small war to make himself look good. He's a militia colonel now, loves to strut about in his fancy uniform from what I hear. Sash and sword, plumed hat, all that nonsense. But any war he starts won't be a short one. Whatever land the tribes have now is all they're ever going to get. They'll fight because there is nothing else they can do. They'd rather live in peace, poor though their lands may be, but Halliday is determined to prod them into an open conflict that can be settled only by military force.''

"Like how?''

Gen. Howard said, "You're too isolated here. Haven't you heard about the so-called incidents that have been taking place in various parts of the territory? So-called renegades sneaking off the reservations to steal horses and cattle, burn bridges and barns, take pot-shots at farmers and stockmen. Six men have been killed so far.''

"I heard something about it,'' Morgan said, "last time I was in Jennings, but that's fifty miles from here. Fact is, I haven't been off this place for two months. What I heard sounded like the usual scrapes. Renegades do sneak off to do a little stealing. Most of the time they're caught or killed.''

Gen. Howard got another cigar going. "These Indians weren't caught or killed because they weren't Indians, I'm pretty sure. Washington may be a long way off, but good people in the territory have been writing to me, telling me what they know or what they suspect. And it all adds up to one thing: Halliday is behind it. I'm telling you Halliday is trying to get people so worked up they'll start killing Indians wherever they find them. And you know where that will lead?''

Morgan didn't think that needed an answer.

Gen. Howard said, ''As more people are killed, maybe even women raped and killed, more places burned, there will be a general outcry for military action. The territorial militia will be called up, the regular army will be forced to move. I'm more afraid of the militia than the army. You know what some of those men are like. Bums, scroungers, thieves, bone-bred killers out for what they can get. You were a militia sergeant yourself before you joined me.''

Morgan didn't like to think very much about the Nez Perce War. It had been no time of glory for him. ''You think it will go that far, sir?''

''I'm convinced of it,'' the general said. ''Something like it happened in West Texas years ago, but there was no real organization behind it. Here there is. Buffalo hunters that were driven off Kiowa land started killing white people, thinking to start a war that would get rid of the Kiowas once and for all. It worked for a while before the hunters were caught and hanged.''

Morgan didn't know what the general wanted him to do, though he had some idea. The Nez Perce War was long in the past, he was ten years older, and all he wanted to do was raise, trade and sell horses. But he knew he would be hard-pressed to turn the general down, no matter what he had in mind.

''But how can Washington let Halliday get away with this?'' Morgan knew the question was bullshit. He just wanted to stay where he was. Things were going good and he wanted to enjoy them. "Doesn't the governor have any say in this?"

Gen. Howard tossed the stub of his cigar into the fire. "The governor is a hack politician with no real power. Anyway, he's firmly under Halliday's thumb, does what he's told. The real power is in Washington, where Halliday has many friends in and out of government, but especially in the War Department and the Bureau of Indian Affairs. He has a highly paid lobbyist, the most corrupt man in Washington—and that's saying something—who spreads the money around. If Halliday wants to crush the Indians and drive them out of Idaho, unless something goes wrong, he's going to do it."

"But where does he want to put them?" Morgan asked.

"Oklahoma, the Indian Territory," the general said. "Halliday thinks there's room enough for them there, which isn't true. Oklahoma is chockful of Indians as it is. Some of them have been there since Andy Jackson started moving Indians around so he could steal their land. Nowadays they have real wooden towns, schools, at least one newspaper, so forth. You can imagine how they'll feel if a lot of uncivilized Idaho Indians start piling in at this late date. You know what will happen."

"A real Indian war," Morgan said, "if they feel crowded."

"Maybe so," the general responded. "And there isn't much I can do to stop this monstrous thing. I'm out of the army and whatever influence I once had is nearly gone. Oh, I have the support of many good people, even a few congressmen and senators, but they don't count, you see. Halliday has money, and how do you fight money?"

"What do you want me to do, General?" Morgan asked.

"Nothing you don't want to do."

Morgan wanted to smile but didn't. For such a godly man his old friend could sling the bullshit pretty good.

"But I think you'll want to help after I explain it," the general went on. "You have a nice place here and you don't want to lose it."

Morgan started to say something, but the general cut in with, "Forgive me, Morgan, I shouldn't have said that. I know you are not a man to be moved by worldly considerations."

Like hell I'm not, Morgan thought, but didn't say.

"I want you to help me stop Halliday," the general said, no longer beating about the bush. "You know this western Idaho country as well or better than any man. I have other men working in other parts of the territory, but this is your home ground, where I want you to see what you can find out. Three so-called incidents have occurred to the south of here, two in the Clearwater Valley, one along the Snake River. A man was killed, a child wounded, a farm burned. The incident on the Snake happened not that far from Lewiston and the town is nervous. You see what I mean?"

The old man wants me to play detective, Morgan thought. In his own interest. If a war spread across the territory there would be no way to keep the Spade Bit out of it. He would rather sit on the porch on Sunday afternoons and drink beer. Not much chance of that now.

"I'll see what I can do," he said, thinking west Idaho was a lot of country, most of it wild. "Where will you be, sir? How can I get hold of you? Information won't mean a thing if you don't get it."

The general massaged the stump of his missing arm, something he did without being aware of it. "That's what worries me," he said. "You can't be in two places at once, scouting around and at the same time getting messages to me. You're going to need a fast rider, someone who knows the country, someone you can trust. Can you think of anyone?"

"Not right off," Morgan said. "The men that work

here do just that—work. None of them signed on to maybe get shot. Sid, my foreman, could do it, but he has to stay here. Place would run down if he wasn't here.''

The general wasn't too pleased. He could be a ruthless old bugger when he wanted to be. ''It's important that you get a good, fast rider before you start out.'' His voice was irritable, but then he smiled. ''Don't mind me I get cranky sometimes.''

You're cranky all the time, Morgan thought, a bit cranky himself. ''I'll think about it.''

Gen. Howard took out his watch and looked at it. ''After I leave here I'll be heading for what's left of the Lapwai reservation to talk to Chief Latah, try to persuade him not to react to provocation. He's no Chief Joseph, but he's the best the western Nez Perce have. That done with, however it goes, I'll be making my way down to Boise. That's where your man can find me, at the Rathdrum Hotel.''

''That's a fair distance,'' Morgan said, thinking how old the general was, how tired he looked now.

The general shifted in his chair. ''Has to be done. Ought to get started right now, but I guess I'll rest a little longer. You ever think about Joseph and the war? No, I guess you don't. I think about it more and more as I get older. Wasn't much of a war, come to think of it: three hundred Nez Perce against five thousand regulars and militiamen. Can you imagine it, we pursued Joseph and his people and turned them back just thirty miles short of the Canadian border. Thirteen-hundred miles and Joseph fought us over every miserable winter mile. Remember the blood on the snow?''

Morgan said nothing and the old man went on. ''If I had to do it over again I would have let them go even if they court-martialed me for it. People thought I was too soft on the Nez Perce. My book about the war, did you read it? I sent you a copy.''

''I read it,'' Morgan said.

"I'm glad somebody did." Gen. Howard ran his hand over his lined face.

Morgan didn't like to see his old friend so dejected. "General," he said, hoping to change the subject, "I've been thinking about how I should proceed. My idea is that I start scouting around for new stock. Not buying exactly, just looking. How does that sound to you?"

The general gave him a sharp look. He didn't miss much. "I think it's better than dressing up as an itinerant preacher." Then he creaked out a laugh. "You're right. It's no use dwelling on the past. You have any idea where you're going to start?"

Morgan said, "Lewiston is the biggest town in these parts. You said there was a bushwhacking near there, the town is jittery. A good kickoff place, I would think."

The general leaned toward the fire as if he didn't want to leave it. "So it is. What you may not know, the Lewiston *City & County News* is owned by Halliday. It's really been beating the war drums since that farmer got killed, his daughter wounded, poor little orphan, the rest of it. Neal, the editor, is a miserable hypocrite."

Something told Morgan he knew more than he was telling. "General, you got somebody working for you in Lewiston, supplying you with information. It would be a help if you told me."

The general took a while to answer; it was quiet in the room except for the crackling of the fire, the voices of the men working outside. "It's a woman," he said at last, "and in her letter she swore me to secrecy. Any reply should be mailed to her as Abigail Meeker, care of her landlady. Guess I'm breaking my word, not that I ever gave it, but you know what I mean. She's terrified of what could happen to her."

Morgan waited.

"Oh, well," the general said. "Her name is Laura Yoder and she's a reporter for Halliday's paper. In her letter, a mighty long one, she wrote what she believes or suspects Halliday is up to. But I'm afraid what she wrote won't be much help to you. That's why I didn't want to bring her into it.''

Morgan was impatient. ''She's not in it, but what did she say?''

''That Halliday is trying to start a war with the Indians. We can skip that. Telegrams have been flying back and forth between Halliday and Neal, the editor, all in some kind of code. More than usual, much more. Neal has been keeping large amounts of cash in his office, so much so that he posts an armed guard there at night. Men she never saw before are in and out of Neal's office, mostly after business hours. Mysterious men were her words.''

Morgan was getting a picture of this nervous biddy: about 40, big teeth, long nose, hair in a bun. ''What was mysterious about them? Did they wear long, black cloaks and masks?''

Gen. Howard clucked his tongue. ''Now, now, Morgan. I'm just telling you what she wrote. I admit she did ramble on a bit, but she's a brave woman just the same. Promise you won't go near her.''

Morgan nodded. ''Whatever you say, sir.'' There had been no need to promise, something that always made him feel foolish, none at all. Putting his trust in a woman who wrote about mysterious men would surely get him killed. ''Anyway, I'd just as soon work on this by myself.''

Gen. Howard got to his feet with an effort. ''Don't forget that good, fast rider.''

''I have a man in mind,'' Morgan said.

''I know he'll be a good one,'' the general said.

Chapter Two

Lying in his blankets nearly ten hours later, listening to Ticknor snoring like a sawmill, Morgan wondered if he wasn't making the biggest mistake of his life. In his time he'd been guilty of some champion fuck-ups. This one could make it into the record books alongside the pie eating contests and Greatest Disasters of History.

Nearby, a creek ran over rocks and it would have been a soothing sound to sleep by if it hadn't been drowned out by Young Ticknor's snoring. It was well past midnight and the wind whistled through the stand of lodgepole pines they were camped in. Even in August it would have been cold at that hour. In late May, the night wind knifed through his two heavy blankets.

Camp was in a hollow, but the wind found you anyway, and it would have been worse higher up the slope that ran down to the creek. The fire had burned down to ash and embers. It should have been built up long since, which was to be Young Ticknor's job, except he hadn't done it.

"Don't you worry, Mr. Morgan," he'd said. "I got a clock in my head that'll alarm me time it needs to be done." Then he'd gone to sleep with his hat on, lying on his side, his back to Morgan.

Morgan sat up, found a small stone, threw it at Young Ticknor's hat. It woke him all right and he rolled out of his blankets with the long-barreled, single-action Colt .45 in his hand, the hammer eared back. Morgan was impressed at how fast it was done. Smooth and fast and silent, no hollering, none of the deep sleeper's bewilderment at the sudden awakening. When he saw Morgan still in his blankets, he eased down the hammer and got to his feet wanting to know what was going on.

"Fix the fucking fire," Morgan told him.

"Sorry, Mr. Morgan," he mumbled. "I'll do it directly."

Morgan lay back with his head against his saddle and closed his eyes. Young Ticknor was still fooling with the fire, but finally it started to blaze up as brush and wood were piled on. He was drifting off to sleep when he felt Young Ticknor standing over him. "What is it you want, kid?"

Young Ticknor had the coffee pot in one hand, a tin cup in the other. "Coffee's still pretty hot, Mr. Morgan, or I can heat it some more. You want a cup?"

"No, Kid, I want to sleep."

Young Ticknor didn't go away. "You want me to sit up with it?"

Morgan raised himself on his elbow. "What're you talking about? Sit up with what?"

"The fire. Case it burns down again. I wouldn't want you to get mad at me."

"The hell with it, get some sleep." Morgan lay back and pulled the blankets up to his chin.

A minute or two later, Young Ticknor was snoring and Morgan was still awake. That kid! The talk with the kid the afternoon of the day before came back to him. It was just after the general waved good-bye and the buckboard rattled off down the road. Young Ticknor looked after it longer than the other men. It took a whistle to get his attention, and when he turned the guilty look was back on his face. "Mr. Morgan, about your boots—"

"Forget about the boots for now. Come in the house, I want to talk to you." Morgan walked ahead of him.

Young Ticknor had been in the house before, but not very often, and he shifted from one foot to the other until Morgan told him to sit down. "Wait," Morgan said, then called Bitsy and told him to fetch a basin of soapy water, a towel, and a pair of clean socks.

"Wha' happen to you nice new boots, boss?" Bitsy asked, the sly old bastard.

Morgan looked at Young Ticknor, who didn't want to meet his eye. "Never mind that," he said to Bitsy. "Just do what I said."

"You betcha, boss." The little Chinaman went away chuckling to himself.

Morgan took off the oily boots, peeled off the socks. "How old are you, kid?"

Young Ticknor looked startled. "Eighteen going on nineteen. Nearer to nineteen. Why'd you want to know, Mr. Morgan?"

Bitsy brought in the basin, the other things, and took away the boots.

"I thought you might be twelve going on thirteen," Morgan said. "The way you fuck things up, I thought you might be about that age. Why do you do it? There has to be a reason."

"You going to fire me, Mr. Morgan?"

"You wouldn't be sitting there if I was."

"You can fire me anytime you like. You don't have to keep me on just because you knew my mother."

"No need to go into that," Morgan said. But the kid

was right. His dead mother was the only reason he was working at Spade Bit. Morgan hadn't seen him for ten years before he turned up three months back, asking for a job. Said he remembered Morgan, the name of his place. Morgan gave him the job and there wasn't a day since he hadn't regretted it.

He looked at the kid sitting awkwardly in the chair, and there was plenty of resemblance to the Betty Ticknor he knew when she was working as a saloon girl at Dyer's Palace in Jennings. Downstairs she cajoled men into buying whiskey; upstairs she serviced the men who wanted a poke, like the three other women who worked there. But unlike the others, she had a kid and lived in a little house—more a shack—owned by Dyer, who charged her rent. The kid was seven or eight at the time.

Morgan saw the kid a few times, didn't give him much thought. Now and then, on her day off, she'd invite Morgan to the house for a fried chicken or baked ham supper. He didn't get to Jennings that often, but when he did he always got hold of Betty Ticknor. She was a fine poke, but they never fucked at her place because the kid was there, all eyes and ears. He had liked her a lot.

She had a little too much chin, like the kid, but she was a good looking woman. Yes sir, a fine fuck and a nice woman. Then the war with Chief Joseph came and when he came back after five months she was dead, shot by a drunken gambler who got clean away, and the kid had gone to live with some uncle. Now, looking at the kid ten years later, he couldn't help but think of her. A shame she had to die like that.

He dried his feet and pulled on the clean socks. Out in the kitchen Bitsy was working on the boots with saddle soap. The kid was cracking his knuckles, something Morgan hated. The kid was a stringbean with crow black hair and long thin hands. Maybe gunfighter's hands. Right now he was looking at the floor.

"Tell me this," Morgan said. "When you mess up your work, is it because you don't like it? Or is it because you're always thinking about something else? I'd like to know."

"I do my best, Mr. Morgan."

"Bullshit! If you were in the army they'd kick your ass. Another thing, what is all this business with guns? I'm as good a shot as you, but I don't work at it all the time."

Young Ticknor showed a little defiance. "You don't clear the holster fast as me."

"No, I don't," Morgan said patiently. "You see, I'm a rancher not a gunman. This craze for gunning didn't just start when you came here."

Young Ticknor looked straight at Morgan. "You want to know about me, is that what you're saying?"

"That's right."

"All right." The kid sat up in his chair. "The man that killed my mother was a drifter gambler that called himself Siddons. Went by other names too. Was said to be quick with a gun. I was a kid when it happened so nothing I could do about it. My uncle, the one that took me in, worked me like a slave, beat me for nothing at all. Always kept a close eye on me so's I couldn't run off. But I did, run off, when I was fourteen. Ran far so he couldn't follow and bring me back. Found work here and there, worst kind of work, me being a kid. Was in Montana, Utah, Nevada, always asking after Siddons. Saved to buy a gun, a good one. I wanted a good gun when I caught up with Siddons. I practiced hard with it. . . ."

Young Ticknor paused but Morgan said nothing.

Then he went on. "Siddons was dead by the time I found his last location. East Helena, Montana. Dead six months, killed in a card game. All I could think to do was piss on his grave."

"Did you?"

"No, I didn't. That would be like what a kid would do. All I wanted was to kill him, square things for my mother, only now I couldn't."

"You never killed anybody," Morgan said.

The kid said, "I could have done it easy if they crossed me bad. Here and there a man would start up, then change his mind."

As the kid talked Morgan could see how a trouble-pushing bully might change his mind. When he talked about how good he was with a gun, there was confidence in his voice. Gone at least for the moment was the fumble-footed kid, and in his place was a man it wouldn't be smart to tangle with. He didn't sound or look dangerous, but there was danger in him.

Morgan puzzled for a bit. "So it's like you prepared yourself for something you wanted gut-aching bad, but it never happened."

This wasn't meant to provoke anger, but it did. The kid looked at Morgan with hard eyes so unlike his usual vacant stare. "You can't blame me for not killing Siddons. I followed him up and down, in and out, of doghouse towns. Not my fault he was dead before I could kill him."

Young Ticknor stopped talking when Bitsy brought in Morgan's boots. The wicked old devil gave the kid a toothless grin, then said to Morgan, "See, boss, good as new, boss. Ladies gonna like them high-steppin' boots."

"Get out of here, you bad old man," Morgan said.

The boots weren't as good as new, but Bitsy had done a good job, with only a few stains remaining. Morgan pulled them on while the kid watched with no expression on his face.

"Looks to me like you're at loose ends. You're working here—you're supposed to be working here—but all you're doing is marking time. For what, if you don't mind telling me?"

19

Young Ticknor had no ready answer. "I don't know, Mr. Morgan."

Morgan said, "If guns are all you know, why don't you work at a gun trade? Get a deputy job, town or county. Join the Texas Rangers, go to work for Wells Fargo, something like that."

"Maybe I will, Mr. Morgan," the kid said. "I'd like to do something."

"Meantime you're no good for ranch work. Look here, you've got to clear your mind of what Siddons did to your mother. It's done, it's over. You can't forget it, I know that, but you've got to look at it from a distance. Can you do that?"

The kid didn't answer the question. Instead he asked, "What's this talk all about, Mr. Morgan?"

Morgan shook his head in exasperation. "Can you straighten up, yes or no? Don't be nodding your head at me. Answer the question."

The kid made as to get up. Morgan told him to sit down.

"Maybe I oughta just quit," the kid said. "Save both of us grief. Like you said, I'm no good at ranch work. Maybe in a few years I'd be all right at it."

In a few hundred years, Morgan thought, not wanting to give up just yet. He needed a rider and the kid was all he had. "Forget about ranch work, kid. I need you for something else. Only here, let me make it plain, if you fuck up you could get me killed, get both of us killed. We'd be doing dangerous work. Now what do you say?"

"My Lord!" the kid said. "That would suit me fine. Forgive me saying it, Mr. Morgan, but ranch work is a pain in the ass. Give me real work and I won't let you down."

Morgan took a breath and told him about Halliday, the rest of it. "If I send a message to Gen. Howard the God-damned thing has to get there. I don't mean get there sometime, not two weeks later than it's supposed to. No stopping off to spark the farm girls, no picking daisies, get it?''

"Got it, Mr. Morgan. And when I'm not riding, I'll be there to watch your back. You don't know how good I am with a gun.''

Morgan wasn't one for sighing, but he felt like it now. "See how you carry on. I'm asking can you do one thing and you want to be doing something else. For the last time—''

"You're the boss,'' the kid said hastily. "You give the orders. You tell me go shoot Halliday and I'll do it.''

"We'll need a good pack horse,'' Morgan said.

Now, ten hours later, Morgan was having second thoughts, lying awake in his blankets when he should be getting his sleep. Fuck it! What was done was done. Look at the bright side, if there was one. Maybe the kid would be all right. If he wasn't, then fuck that too. He would just have to wait and see.

Morgan slept fine after that and it wasn't till he smelled coffee and frying bacon that he opened his eyes. First light was glimmering through patches of fog and it was damp and cold. The stink of bobcat was in the air, but nowhere close to camp. He hadn't made a sound, but the kid turned the moment he was awake. The fucker had eyes in the back of his head, it looked like. He was hunkered down beside the fire, holding the fry pan, turning the bacon in it with a fork.

"I got everything ready,'' he said.

"Good.'' Morgan started to roll up his blankets. "Watch the bacon. It's starting to burn.''

Morgan tied his bedroll and led the two saddle horses and the pack horse down to the creek to drink. He splashed water in his face and rubbed it round the back of his neck. Birds were chirping in the white firs that grew along the edge of the creek. He took the horses back up the slope and tethered them.

The kid set out plates of bacon, beans and biscuits. Morgan took care not to hold his cup while the kid filled it with piping hot coffee. The bacon wasn't burned too bad and the coffee was ink-black strong, the way he liked it. "We should make the north fork of the Clearwater by afternoon. You know the way?"

The kid said no.

It had rained during the night and the grass under the trees was wet. Morgan sat on his saddle, so did the kid. "We'll stay with the river till it gets to Lewiston. After that, I don't know. Maybe we'll look around, listen to what they're saying in the saloons. Drink a few beers. Find a room for the night. Any talking to be done I'll do it, all right?"

Young Ticknor said seriously, "All right. Only thing I will not do is drink beer."

"Why not? Have you been listening to Gen. Howard?"

"No, sir. Beer makes me wild, is the trouble."

"Well, we don't want you going wild. Forget the beer and pay attention. Like I told you, we're on a look-see trip. Interested in new stock. Maybe we're buying, maybe we're not. That's all you have to say if we get separated and somebody asks questions."

"You think they'll have their suspicions of us? Halliday's people?"

"It doesn't have to be Halliday's people. A wrong answer could get back to people that work for him, people that support him. Stop eyeing what's left of the bacon, eat it so we can be off."

Breakfast was over and Young Ticknor was scouring the fry pan with a wet rag and a handful of creek sand. Taking too long to do it, Morgan thought, but he couldn't keep riding the kid all the time.

"Mr. Morgan," the kid said. "These bushwhackers

Halliday is dressing up as Injuns. The ones that shot the little girl down by Lewiston. How could they do something like that?"

"It would be as easy as shooting a sick dog. Nothing so bad people won't do it."

Young Ticknor dried the pan and stowed it away with the rest of the gear. That was the last of the housekeeping. Morgan wanted to be gone. "I wouldn't mind killing them," the kid said. "They should be made to pay for it."

Morgan threw the saddle over his horse and tightened the cinch. "You're right, but I doubt they will. Justice isn't just blind; it's hard of hearing and has a gimpy leg."

The kid was saddling his own horse. "I can't believe that, Mr. Morgan."

Morgan didn't say there had been no justice for his mother. "Believe what you like. Get a move on. We should be miles gone from here."

But once they got started they made good time. The sun came up hot and burned off the fog. There was no trail, but Morgan knew this country and it was an easy ride, downhill most of the way. They crossed meadows bright with flowers, forded some deep creeks, and got to the river about three o'clock. Here they rested the animals, chewed biscuits, drank cold coffee from a canteen. After that they saddled up and started to follow the river west, following the old trail made thirty years before. But it wasn't like following a river in flat country like Kansas. Sometimes the trail ran so high you lost sight of the river. Sometimes it ran close. Whatever it did, it was the fastest way to get to Lewiston from Spade Bit. Better time could be made if you could cross the wide, deep, fast-flowing river. No way to do that. So you had to stay with all its twists and turns until it took you right to the north end of the town.

They still had a good way to go when it started to get

dark. Rolling black clouds threatened to crack open and let loose a downpour that could go on for hours. It took a while to find a rock overhang that would provide some protection for the horses and themselves. They were gathering deadwood for the fire when the rain started, falling straight down instead of being wind blown, but it wasn't too bad under the overhang. It was tolerable even when an occasional gust of wind blew cold rain in on top of them, soaking them good and threatening to put out the fire. Water ran down a crack in the rocks and made a pool the horses drank from.

Morgan did the cooking with his back to the rain. Nothing shittier in the world than bacon and beans floating in an inch of water. The rain came down cold and steady, as if it would never stop. The kid had his own sack of brown sugar and he heaped it into his coffee until it must have been like drinking hot molasses. Morgan always wondered at people who spoiled good black coffee with sugar.

"Mr. Morgan," the kid said. "You remember what I said about killing Drick Halliday?"

"I thought that was just a way of talking," Morgan said.

"Not a bit of it. It would stop this Injun war before it got started. You said yourself he's the brains. With him dead it would just fizzle out."

"No doubt it would, but you can't do it."

"Course I could do it. I'm near as good with a rifle as I am a sixer."

"I didn't mean you couldn't kill him, killing he surely deserves, but you can't do it. Gen. Howard wouldn't like it. We're working for him, remember, so put it out of your mind. Clean up and get some sleep."

Morgan checked on the horses before he turned in. The kid hadn't said anything more about killing Halliday, but Morgan knew he was thinking about it. After he scoured and rinsed the dishes he sat by the fire cleaning and oiling his long-barreled Colt .45. Rolled in his blankets, Morgan watched him through half-closed eyes. Now and then he'd raise the pistol and sight along the barrel, no doubt seeing Drick Halliday at the other end. It would be a bitch if he went after Halliday on his own. Halliday's powerful friends might not want to go ahead with his war plan, but they'd do their damnedest to find out who was behind the killing. The kid would be linked to him and he'd be linked to Gen. Howard. A determined lawman could do it. Even if they couldn't prove anything, it would be very sad for the general to end his days under a cloud of suspicion.

Morgan knew he'd need to have another talk with the kid, a tough talk that would penetrate even his thick skull. Kill Halliday and you'll have me to deal with, would be the message.

The kid was still sitting by the fire, still fooling with the .45, when Morgan dropped off to sleep.

They got to Lewiston before noon the next day.

Chapter Three

Lewiston, at the junction of the Snake and Clearwater Rivers, was a long one-street town walled in by mountains. Here the Clearwater was swallowed by the Snake, which twisted its way west into Washington. They called Lewiston Idaho's only seaport. Ocean-going steamers came up the Columbia and the Snake right to its door. Morgan always thought it was strange to see ships so far from the sea. The ships brought brawling sailors, hard cases, and wanted men from all over. Between them they gave the town a well earned reputation for lawlessness.

They crossed the bridge that spanned the Clearwater at the north end of town. It was warm here after the chill winds of the high country. Thick stands of pine grew along the slopes of the mountains that loomed over the town. It was a busy town, choked with ore and lumber and farm wagons, and no one paid them any attention.

Morgan liked this town, not that he got there very often. When he had money and time enough, San Francisco was

26

where he kicked up his heels. Never much of a drinker except for beer, he did his heel kicking in the Frisco whorehouses. Lewiston was nowhere as good in that line, but it was better than all right. There was no end of whorehouses here, ranging from cribs to fancy-pants places. The sailors, always free with their money, had to be serviced; so did the miners and the lumbermen, the cowhands from the ranches. Whorehouses and saloons stayed open night and day, and if Lewiston wasn't as wild as Dodge City in its heyday, it was wild enough.

It gladdened Morgan's heart to see so many whores on parade. In Lewiston they always did their stroll on their day off, something you saw in no other town. Nobody bothered them. The law was strict about that. The law and the saloonkeepers and whorehouse owners were in close alliance. So if you wanted to sample the merchandise, you couldn't do it in the street.

Young Ticknor was gaping at the whores and Morgan wondered if he was thinking of his mother, the dead whore. "What did you say?" he asked, turning toward Morgan.

"First we'll stable the horses, is what I said. Then we'll hunt up a room."

Morgan knew the stable and the room would cost him plenty. So far from everywhere, Lewiston was a high-priced town where you paid up or did without.

"Then I'm going to drink three or four mugs of good San Francisco beer. It comes here by boat."

On their way to the livery stable they passed the brick building that housed the *City & County News* and Morgan thought of Laura Yoder, the lady reporter who'd written to Gen. Howard. Morgan hadn't changed his picture of her. About 40, long nose, fussy manner, hair in a severe bun. Morgan knew he could be wrong, but he didn't think so. Just the same, there weren't that many lady reporters around, so there had to be some good reason why she held the job she did. Ten-to-one she nagged people so bad they answered her questions just to get rid of her.

They stabled the horses and found a small, bare room in a boarding house. There was only one bed and Morgan told Young Ticknor he could sleep on the floor. "I don't care," the kid said. "One time in a snowstorm I slept in a shithouse, all that was left of a place that burned down. Shithouse was old and dry so it wasn't too bad. Another time. . . . "

"All right," Morgan told him. "You can sleep in the bed. Just keep to your side of it, no kicking or rolling around. Now listen to me because I won't say it again. This bullshit about killing Halliday. . . . "

Morgan laid down the law about Halliday. "This is a town where he has strong support, so he could be here. He owns the newspaper and other businesses. If he is here, don't even think about killing him. Kill Halliday and you'll be hanging from a beam five minutes later. That is, if I don't kill you myself."

"I hear what you're saying, Mr. Morgan," the kid said cheerfully.

"All right," Morgan said. "Let's go down and you can watch me drink beer. We'll wander a bit, then maybe see what's happening in the whorehouses. I know one place pretty good. I saw you looking at the ladies. What do you think?"

"I think I might like it."

"You sound like you never poked a woman."

"You're wrong there, Mr. Morgan. I poked hundreds in my time."

Morgan had to smile at him. "That's more than I can say. Let's go, I'm thirsty."

It was just past one o'clock, but all the saloons were doing a busy daytime trade. The first place they went into was crowded but orderly, and some of the credit for that must have been due to the presence of a huge, bearded man who sat on a high stool, a pick handle stuck in his belt. No music here, no saloon girls, no gaming tables in back, it was a place for men who just wanted to drink. Some mannerly pushing took them to the bar, where Morgan ordered three mugs of beer. One he set in front of the kid for the sake of appearances. In a saloon like this a man who didn't drink could easily find himself being laughed at. Morgan didn't want that to happen. It would not be smart to laugh at the kid, but a man with booze in his brain might not know that.

Morgan drank all three beers and felt better for it. "We'd best be moving on," he told Young Ticknor. "Place must have changed owners, all miners now."

On the way out a man Morgan didn't know clapped him on the back and wanted to know how he was keeping himself. "You're Morgan, am I right? You don't remember me? Henry Lattimer is who I am. You were in my old militia outfit before you transferred to scouting for the general. How about a drink for old times sake?" Lattimer was a big man built like a rain barrel.

"Maybe later," Morgan said. "Got some business to attend to."

"Good luck to you," Lattimer said. "Somebody told me you were doing real good in the horse business." Lattimer smiled but his eyes were angry.

Morgan wasn't pleased to be recognized so quickly. Hell, it wasn't like he was such a regular visitor to this town. His brief fame as a scout for Gen. Howard was ten years in the past and should have been long forgotten by now. So it had to be a fluke. He wanted to believe it was a fluke. Best if he could just poke around with nobody putting a name to his face.

"Time for more beer," he said to Young Ticknor.

A man and a woman were standing on the steps of the newspaper building as they went past. Morgan recognized the man, rail-thin and middleaged, as Simon Darcy Neal,

29

editor of the *City & County News*. Neal had been a militia captain in the war. Morgan thought Neal looked at him longer than was necessary, but couldn't be sure. He was sure he'd never spoken to the man.

The woman with him was young and beautiful, and the slight hardness in her face took nothing away from her good looks. How old she was he couldn't say. Maybe not as young as she appeared, probably about thirty-five. She had reddish brown hair and was taller than Neal by several inches, which made her about five-nine. She could be Neal's wife, but he didn't think so. They just didn't go together. More likely she was the wife of some local big-wig. Morgan passed her with only one thought in his mind and that was how much he'd like to fuck her. But that was wishful thinking: it wasn't going to happen.

They were in a saloon next to the town hall when she came in, not right after them, about five minutes later. This was a place favored by lawyers, politicians and businessmen. It was quieter and the drinks cost more. Morgan and Young Ticknor were at a table and when she came in she walked right over. Every man there looked after her.

"My name is Laura Yoder," she said. "I'm a reporter for the *City & County News*. May I sit down?"

Morgan stood up and pulled out a chair for her. "What can I do for you, Miss Yoder?" So much for the picture he'd formed of the lady reporter.

"You're Lee Morgan, aren't you?" she said. "Mr. Neal was sure he recognized you. You passed us a few minutes ago."

Morgan was still on his feet. "Would you like something to drink?" He wanted a minute or two to think.

"A small glass of beer."

Morgan came back with the beer, placed it in front of her, and sat down. Young Ticknor couldn't keep his eyes off her. Small wonder: she was something to look at all right.

"Fire away," Morgan said.

Laura Yoder took a leather covered notebook from the side pocket of her coat. "Mr. Neal says you were chief scout for Gen. Howard during the Nez Perce War of ten years ago. That being so, I would like to know what you think of the recent attacks on whites by Indians in this territory. A number have been reported, as I'm sure you are aware. Do you think such incidents will lead to a general Indian uprising such as you had here in 1877?"

Morgan looked at her. "There haven't been any up where I live."

"That wasn't the question, Mr. Morgan."

Morgan knew he had to be careful. This saloon was quieter than most and everybody there was trying to listen in.

"There could be an Indian war," he said, "if these attacks keep up. It doesn't take much to start one."

He thought that ought to hold her, but it didn't. "If there is a war, will you be putting on your old scout's uniform? You were quite a famous scout in the last war."

"Scouts don't wear uniforms, Miss Yoder. But the answer to your question is, I don't know. The war hasn't happened yet. Like everybody else, I'll have to wait and see."

Laura Yoder showed some impatience or pretended to. "That's a pretty vague answer, Mr. Morgan."

Damn! She smelled good and he felt his cock stir. "Sorry I can't be more definite, Miss Yoder. All I can say is I'll do my duty when the time comes. Got to be going now."

"Must you?" Laura Yoder got up too. "I have something else I'd like to ask you."

"No time right now." Morgan started for the door with Young Ticknor trailing along behind.

31

Outside, Young Ticknor said, "Here she comes. She's fixing to follow us to the next place. I wish she'd follow me."

Morgan grinned at him. "She's not going to follow me anyplace right now. I'm going up to the room to take a nap. You better do the same. I don't want her pumping you."

The kid looked down the bustling street, at the whores still on their day-off stroll. "But I don't want to take a nap, Mr. Morgan. I'll be fine, she'll get nothing out of me."

Morgan pointed. "You need a nap. Come on now. You may be a smart fella, but that is a sly looking woman and will keep after you."

They went up to the room and Morgan stretched out on the bed, thinking of Laura Yoder. What in hell was she up to? Hard to say. Maybe just trying to fill up her notebook, maybe not. He wondered if Neal had sent her after him. No doubt he had, but that didn't have to mean anything in itself. There had been a few newspaper stories about him at the time of the old war. Well, fuck Neal and fuck her. But when he thought about it, he'd rather fuck her than Neal. Getting to do it was a remote possibility. Remote as it could get.

The kid sat on a rickety chair and cracked his knuckles, hating to be cooped up in the middle of the day. Morgan didn't blame him: after three months at the ranch he wanted to be out seeing the sights. But there was no help for it. If this Laura Yoder got at him, a few wrong answers could land them in trouble. It was possible that her letter to Gen. Howard had been a phony, something calculated to draw out the old man, learn something of his plans. No way to know what she was. But spy or honest reporter, she had the face of a foxy angel and an ass just made for squeezing.

There was a knock on the door and the kid looked at

Morgan. "See who it is," Morgan said.

The kid opened the door with one hand on his gun. It was Laura Yoder, not a bit flustered, and she said, "Tell Mr. Morgan he won't get away from me that easily."

"Come in, Miss Yoder," Morgan said from the bed. There was a way to get rid of her if that's what he wanted to do. Thinking about it, maybe he didn't. He might get more out of her than she'd get out of him.

The kid opened the door to let her in and the sight of Morgan lying there with a bulge in his pants didn't even make her blink. Out came the notebook and the pencil, the tools of her trade. She sat on the only chair in the room and put on a professional air.

"Now, Mr. Morgan," she started off again.

"I'd think this would be bad for your reputation, Miss Yoder," Morgan said. "Coming up here like this, alone, two men in a room. Lord knows what people will think."

"I'm a reporter. I go anywhere I have to. People don't think anything about it. It's part of the job. It's as if I'm invisible and have no sex."

"Not possible." Morgan raised up. "You're not invisible to me." A thought occurred to him and he told the kid to go down and get something to eat.

Young Ticknor was always ready to eat, but not this time. "I ain't hungry, Mr. Morgan."

"Sure you are. Go on now," Morgan said firmly.

The kid went out and Morgan smiled at Laura Yoder. "Just the two of us, Miss Yoder. Mind if I call you Laura?"

"Call me anything you like. My next question is what are you doing in Lewiston?"

"Looking around for new stock. If I see something I like I'll buy it. If I don't, I'll pass. Why all this interest in me?"

She ignored the question. "I'd think you'd be staying

close to home at a time like this. If an Indian war breaks out you'll be—''

"Caught with my pants down? You're an emanciated woman. You must know the expression.''

"You can't shock me, Mr. Morgan. I've seen everything. I would like to know what you're doing in Lewiston? What about an honest answer? Are you spying around for Gen. Howard?''

"Gen. Howard!'' Morgan turned on his side to look at her. "I haven't seen the general since the war. He could be dead for all I know.''

Laura Yoder moved from the chair to the edge of the bed. The movement seemed natural enough: the determined reporter wanting to get closer to her subject. And after all, if he could believe her, she had been in a lot worse places than this. The light fragrance that came from her made him hornier than any heavy perfume. She had green eyes, hard and clever, but lovely just the same.

"You know the general isn't dead, Mr. Morgan. It's even rumored that he's back here in Idaho, doing what he can to head off this war. I'm on his side, Mr. Morgan, and I'll do anything I can to help. You can trust me. Is he here and are you working for him?''

"So you can write it up for Halliday's paper?''

"No, I just want to know. If you are working for him, there are things I can tell you. But how can I trust you if you won't trust me.''

Morgan reached for her and she came into his arms without a struggle. He knew some ambitious reporters would do anything to get a story, but this was carrying it pretty far. Or maybe she just wanted cock. No matter to him which it was. After months without a woman his cock was like an iron bar. He'd fuck her blind and still not tell her anything. He hoped she wouldn't be too disappointed. But nobody had asked her to follow him around. If she wanted to spread her legs, as a reporter or as a woman, that was her business.

Getting her clothes off was no trouble at all, she helped him to do it. She was a lanky woman and her breasts were on the small side, but had the look of ripe pears. She was well muscled and maybe she took a lot of exercise like these emancipated women were said to do. There was a lovely smell to her: lemon soap and toilet water. This one didn't just take a bath on Saturday night. Morgan had such a hard-on that he got out of his clothes like they were on fire. He wanted to get into her so bad that he didn't even get up to lock the door. If the kid came back too soon, let him get an eyeful.

He tried to get on top of her and spread her legs, but she balked at that. What the hell was she up to?

"I'm going to put a sheath on you," she told him matter of factly. "I don't want to get pregnant, it would ruin everything. Have you ever worn a sheath?"

Morgan knew what a sheath was. They made them out of scraped sheep intestines. They were supposed to fit your cock like a second skin. He didn't like the idea.

"I've never worn one and I don't want to wear one now." That was telling her.

She pulled away from him and he didn't try to stop her. If she decided to yell for help, he'd be up on a rape charge. Popular lady reporter attacked by brutal rancher.

"No sheath, no sex," she said. "Look. You're a big boy. It won't hurt you."

"What if I promise to pull out in time?"

"Men say that all the time, but they don't do it. They get carried away at the last moment. I'd love to have you in me, Morgan, but I can't afford to take a chance. Listen. It feels just the same."

Morgan resigned himself to fucking with a second skin on his cock. Anything to slide his cock into this beautiful creature. "All right," he said.

She had the damn thing in a little leather case in her pocket. Always come prepared, he thought. It looked like an empty sausage casing, which it was in a way. His cock was standing straight up so it was no trouble to get it on. She did it expertly as if she'd done it many times before. She gave his cock a squeeze after she pulled the sheath down all the way.

"See how easy it was."

"Yup."

Morgan spread her legs and slid his cock into her. She was hot and juicy and it was like putting it into a jar of warm honey. It felt so good that he forgot about the thing on his cock. He drove in and out of her like a piston, thinking this is what he'd been missing all those womanless months at the ranch.

She wrapped her long legs around the small of his back, pulling him tighter into her. She kissed him passionately, as if she loved him very much. Her tongue probed into his mouth and he sucked on it. Her cunt contracted and relaxed. She knew exactly how to do it. Morgan gave her long thrusts that made her quiver all over. He could feel the hot juice leaking out of her, wetting the bed under her.

"Oh, you're a wonderful lover," she whispered. "I'm going to come in a minute and I want you to come with me. It's so good when a man and a woman come together." And with that her cunt seemed to take on a life of its own. It tightened up so much he could barely move his cock. Her come was so violent that she nearly threw him off the bed. She kept trying to raise up, but he pinned her firmly to the bed, shoved his cock in all the way and shot his load. Months of stored up come volleyed into her. Into the sheath, he thought, suddenly remembering what was on his cock. She was right: it felt the same, it didn't make any difference.

"We'll rest for a while," she whispered, gently shoving him off her. "And when you're ready we'll do it again.

And then we'll rest and do it again. I could do it all day."

"So could I." Morgan was quite sincere about that.

Snuggling up to him she whispered, "I feel as if I've known you all my life. I have such a feeling of trust in you. Do you have the same feeling about me. I hope you do."

"I do." Morgan didn't trust her as far as he could throw her. Not that he wanted to throw her anywhere. It was nice to have her beside him in bed.

She reached down to play with his cock, the sheath still on it. "Then why won't you tell me if you're working for Gen. Howard? I want to help him. I wrote him a letter about Halliday, but he didn't write back. I hate Halliday."

"I guess a lot of people do. But I'm not working for the general and against Halliday. These days I'm just a horse rancher. I wish you'd believe me."

Now she was playing with his balls. "I don't believe you and it makes me sad. I know you're working for Gen. Howard no matter how much you deny it, and I'm going to give you some information you can pass on to him."

Morgan didn't know what to think. "Well, I'll listen."

"Halliday is bringing hired gunmen in from San Francisco. I heard Neal talking to the man who's been recruiting them. It was in the evening and I'd come back to get my notebook. They were in Neal's office and they didn't hear me come in. Neal is one of Halliday's favorites so he's arrogant and careless, thinking who can harm him?"

Morgan wasn't sure he believed her. There were plenty of gunmen in Idaho. Why import killers from San Francisco? But maybe Halliday didn't want locals who might talk too much. Anyway, he'd pass the information on to the general and let him decide how much it was worth.

"You don't seem too interested," she said irritably when he didn't say anything. "Well, here's something that ought to shake you up. Halliday's agents, his go-betweens, have been giving guns to the Indians. Small shipments to those who want them. Three weeks ago a young Indian from Father Boudreau's mission came to talk to Neal. One of Halliday's go-betweens was with him. The young Indian wanted guns, not to be used against whites, but against Indians at the mission who were too loyal to the stinking priest, as he called him. The young Indian wanted to get rid of the priest and the boot-lickers. He spoke good English. Neal said he could supply the guns provided there would be no killing of white settlers. If there was a war, the mission Indians need not be drawn into it. Mr. Halliday's demand for the removal of all Indians need not apply to them. Campaign talk, Neal said. Intelligent Indians had to take what Halliday said with a grain of salt."

"Tricky stuff," Morgan said.

"They were lying to each other," Laura Yoder said. "You know where Father Boudreau's mission is?"

"The Salmon River country, far back there. I've heard of it. It's been in the paper from time to time. Father Boudreau got special permission to start a mission with people from the Lapwai reservation north of here. Wanted to make it an experiment, see what the Nez Perce were capable of. All they had on the reservation was idleness, drunkenness, and despair."

"You're remarkably well informed."

"I read the papers. Father Boudreau's mission aroused a lot of hostility when he first started up. Most people thought the Nez Perce ought to stay on the reservation where they belonged. There were editorials condemning it, fiery speeches by politicians."

"I wasn't here then," Laura Yoder said. "I think that young Indian wants the guns to get rid of the priest and the sub-chief who came with them to the mission. His name is Notus, which means 'It is all right' in their language. He is an old man, very loyal to Father Boudreau."

It could be true, Morgan thought. There were always

hotheads among the tribes, young firebrands wanting to prove themselves in battle. Braves who dreamed of the glory days when men were warriors and mighty hunters, not tame farmers. Most of them were assholes and their dreams were bullshit. But the memory of the Custer massacre still nagged at them.

Morgan fucked Laura Yoder, but this time she was sullen and irritable because he had not responded to what she'd told him. Too bad about that. He had hoped to fuck her all day and maybe all night. The kid could get another room someplace. But the way she was, there was no chance of that. Morgan fucked her with great enthusiasm, knowing her anger would soon break loose.

It did, right after he shot his load for the second time. She came herself, but it seemed to make her angry. She had been giving him her best and he hadn't given her an inch. An inch of information, that is.

"I'm very disappointed in you," she said, pulling the sheath off his cock. Vindictively, she squeezed his come out on the sheet and stowed the sheath away in its leather case. To be washed later, Morgan thought.

"I'm sorry," Morgan said, "but I have nothing to tell you. If I had, I would. Honest."

She actually jumped off the bed and got dressed fast. "Go to hell, you miserable liar."

She slammed the door on the way out.

Chapter Four

Morgan got dressed and went downstairs to look for the kid. He found him sitting on the porch, cleaning his nails with a pocket knife.

"That Miss Yoder looked plenty mad when she went out just now." The kid didn't smile. "Guess you two didn't hit it off. Too bad, she's a honey."

"So she is. Let's go get our usual two glasses of beer. I want to talk to you. Did you eat?"

The kid stood up. "Sure I did. The prices they charge in this town!"

"Don't fret. I'll make it up to you. Come on."

There was no sign of Laura Yoder, which didn't mean she wasn't keeping an eye on him. Even after fucking her he still hadn't figured her out. The information about the guns could be bullshit, even if she believed it herself. For all her hard, professional manner there was something fanciful about her. If she wanted something to be true, then it was true. On the other hand, the story about the guns could be a clever way of sending him on a wild goose chase, something to divert him from his main work of finding out what Halliday was up to.

They went into a saloon and Morgan paid for two beers which he took to a table that three men were just leaving. This was a big, loud place. It even had a band blaring away on a platform built above the bar. Some of the drinkers were sailors off the ships. Morgan saw no familiar faces, for which he was thankful.

Fucking always made him thirsty, and he drank the first mug of beer in a few gulps. There was so much noise, the kid had to lean forward to hear what Morgan was saying. But the noise had a good side to it, nobody could listen in.

Morgan told the kid about the guns and all he did was nod. "It may be a bullshit story, but we have to go down there and take a look. If Halliday's agents are slipping guns to some Indians it could mean real trouble for all the tribes. What's to stop him from saying the Indians have been gathering and hiding guns all along, planning a war, just waiting for the right time to start it."

Young Ticknor had a good question. "But how are we to find the guns if they're hid?"

"We won't be looking for the guns," Morgan said. "What we're going to do is ride down there and I'll talk to the missionary. His name is Boudreau, I've heard of him. He knows his Indians better than anybody. Maybe he can tell us something."

The kid leaned forward even more. "Would be a funny place to be bringing guns, an Indian mission? I would say a reservation would be more likely. That's where you'll find the wild ones that don't want to be there. Guns to them would look good."

The kid was speaking nothing less than the truth. Just the same, it had to be checked. From what he'd heard, the mission Indians were happy enough. This Father

Boudreau treated them well, didn't preach at them too hard, not like the Baptist and Methodist missionaries in other parts of the territory. A tough man who had been an army chaplain at one time, he protected them from the Indian-hating settlers and ran off the whiskey sellers when they came around with their rotgut wares. Nobody had to stay at the mission if they didn't want to. Any man could go back to the regular Indian Bureau reservation where life was bleak, food supplies were scarce, and there was no comfort of any kind. As far as Morgan knew, nobody had done so. And the old chief himself, Notus, was a good Catholic and content to remain where he was.

Young Ticknor was drawing pictures on the beer-wet table with his finger. "They ain't going to tell the priest about the guns. If they're doing it, they prob'ly bring them in while he's away someplace, then hide them good. The guilty ones will deny it."

"No doubt they will at first," Morgan said. "But Father Boudreau has the reputation of being a very hard man. As smart as he's hard. Anyway, Indians are bad liars. They don't have the training we do. I'm thinking Father Boudreau will know if they're lying. If he decides they're lying, if he thinks they have guns hidden, then you've got to head for Boise to inform Gen. Howard. If he hasn't gotten there yet, wait for him. Leave no messages, you hear?"

"I hear you plain. But how do I find you later?"

Morgan picked up the second beer mug. "We have to figure that out."

He was drinking the last of the beer when Lattimer, the man he'd seen earlier, came in with two other men. All three were drunk, Lattimer more so than the others. Lattimer was a big man and his companions were big enough. Morgan couldn't remember a lot about Lattimer. He thought he was a small rancher who did some farming on the side. Poor men did that to make ends meet. If they'd ever talked, had a drink together, he had no memory of it. He sure as hell didn't want to talk or drink with him now.

Lattimer had other ideas, and there was something ugly about the way he bulled through the crowd. Morgan and Young Ticknor were getting up when he got to the table.

"You're not leaving, are you, Morgan?" Lattimer's tone of voice made it plain that he didn't want Morgan to leave, would do something to stop him if he tried. "You wouldn't drink with me before. Why was that? Too good to drink with a poor man like me? You, the big horse rancher that hobnobs with generals, sits in their tent drinking coffee with them while the rest of us stand out in the rain."

Morgan tried to make a joke out of it. The last thing he wanted was a fight. "When a general offers you coffee, you drink it. That or face a firing squad."

It didn't work. Lattimer was in no mood to be fobbed off with lame jokes. "You were never in danger of that, Morgan. The general's fair-haired boy is what you were. You didn't have a pot to piss in when the war came. How did things change so much for the good? Did you get lucky or did the general set you up in business? The two of you always talking, drinking coffee. Mighty queer if you ask me."

Morgan knew what he meant. So did the two men with him, and they laughed. The kid didn't do anything, just stood there with a deadpan face, his hand not too far from his gun. Oh Christ, Morgan thought, these three fools are unarmed and the kid is ready to kill them.

Lattimer pushed in a bit closer. His belly was as big as he was. His two friends moved in when he did. Lattimer socked a meaty fist into the palm of his other hand.

"Sit down and have a drink, Morgan. We'll drink beer and you can tell us how you got to be such a big horse rancher. Sit down before I sit you down. You and this string bean kid, sit down!''

The kid's quiet voice cut through the noise. ''Don't you be calling me names, mister. I don't like it.''

''Oho! He doesn't like it! The beanpole doesn't like it.'' Lattimer elbowed one of the men in the ribs. The man laughed, but he was watching the kid, more mindful of him than Lattimer was. Lattimer thought the kid was just that, and he kept mouthing off. ''He doesn't like it, but what's he going to do about it? Got a big gun on his hip and is looking daggers at me. Am I supposed to be scared? Course I am, only I ain't. I think I'll take that big gun away from this kid.''

Young Ticknor moved back a pace. ''Don't try it, mister.''

Morgan knew Lattimer was a whisker away from being killed. ''Go easy, Lattimer,'' he said. ''It's me you've been pushing.''

Lattimer talked without looking at him. ''I'll get back to you. Right now I got to deal with this snotnose. Let's have the gun, kid. Hand it over and I won't hurt you.''

Morgan did the only thing he could to save Lattimer's life. He hit him as hard as he could, not in the jaw, which was like a rock, but in the gut. The blow would have sunk another man to the floor. Lattimer just grunted and swung around to give Morgan all his attention. Men close by began to yell. A fight was always good entertainment. Lattimer crowded in with the two men behind him.

The kid's gun came out like a flash and he said, ''You two keep out of it. Three against one ain't fair.''

The two men stayed back and the kid holstered his gun. Morgan was watching the kid too closely to see Lattimer's big fist swinging at his face. It took him squarely in the cheekbone and knocked him back across the table. The table went over and he went with it. His cheekbone wasn't split, but it felt like it was. Lattimer didn't kick him or hit him with a chair. Instead, he made beckoning gestures with both hands.

"You can lay in the spit or get up, *Mister* Morgan. Get up and I'll knock you down again. I'll keep knocking you down till I get tired of it. You, too."

Lattimer hiccuped and thought it was funny. The men with him didn't laugh. They had seen the kid's gun action. "Come on, Henry," one of them said, "this has gone far enough."

Lattimer ignored him and the crowd liked that. Some of them began to give Morgan advice, like spectators at a prize fight. Lattimer grinned and raised his two big fists above his head. Morgan came at him fast an i butted him in the gut. This had some effect, but he didn't go down. All he did was stagger back and that made him mad because men were hooting and laughing.

His red face turned mean and dangerous. "I'm going to stomp you," he roared.

He bored in fast for such a big man, both fists swinging like sledgehammers. The crowd was yelling now, wanting to see blood spilled. Morgan was a pretty good saloon brawler, but it would take a lot of work to put this big bastard on the floor. He tried to keep his temper and didn't succeed. Here he was, minding his own business, and this stupid bastard that he barely knew wouldn't let him be. His hand moved toward his gun, but he didn't touch it. This didn't call for gunplay.

Lattimer swung at his head and missed. Morgan tried to kick him in the balls, but he jerked to one side and took the kick in the thigh. Lattimer roared more from anger than pain. "Now we're kicking, are we? I'll show you kicking."

This was brag because Lattimer was too heavy to do much fast kicking. But he'd be a right good stomper if he got a man down. Those thick legs and heavy boots would flatten a man like a chicken steak. He came at

Morgan again, trying to crowd him in against the wall. He swung at Morgan's face and broke the wood facing of the wall instead. The splintered wood tore his hand and it came away dripping blood. Bones in that hand must have been broken, but he was too drunk or too mad to feel pain. He felt it quick enough when he landed a wild punch to the side of Morgan's head. The blow stunned Morgan for a moment without doing any real damage. Lattimer roared like a bull as the pain from the bad hand shot up his arm. But it didn't put him out of action. He switched to the left hand and he wasn't half as good with that. He came at Morgan again, the bad hand hanging down, the other one making wild swings.

Morgan backed away from him, thinking where the hell were the fucking bouncers. The crowd was still yelling, so were the bartenders, for all the good it did them. The hell of it was the band kept on playing, adding to the din. Morgan felt like a fool to be caught up in something like this. It was time to finish it and get out of there.

Backing up, he nearly fell over a chair and it took a stagger to right himself. His hand closed over the back of the sturdy chair and he swung it around in front of him. Lattimer was still coming after him. Morgan swung the heavy chair above his head with both hands and smashed Lattimer on top of the skull with it. Morgan put all his strength behind the blow and Lattimer looked as if he'd been poleaxed, but he didn't go down right away. He stood stock still for an instant, then his eyes glazed over and he sank to the floor.

Somebody in the crowd yelled, "Watch it! Watch it!" Another voice, a city voice, said "Cheese it! Here comes trouble!"

Two thick-bodied men with the marked-up faces of old prizefighters were shoving their way through the mob of gawkers. Both carried short ash clubs, smooth and polished by constant handling. Lattimer, lying bloody on the floor, might have been a sack of spuds for all they cared.

"Out," one of them said to Morgan.

"Yes sir, we're going right out," Morgan said. "Come on, kid."

He turned but hadn't gone two feet before he was seized by the collar of his coat, the seat of his pants, rushed through the crowd, and pitched into the street.

Behind him he heard the kid yelling, "Lay a hand on me and I'll fucking kill you. I fucking mean it."

Morgan was picking himself up when the kid came out of the saloon under his own steam. Next came Lattimer, dumped on the sidewalk like a bale of hay. Lattimer's two friends had made themselves scarce. Now they were back, trying to revive their fallen friend.

Morgan dusted himself off. No broken bones at any rate. People had already lost interest. Men getting chucked out of saloons happened all the time in Lewiston. Morgan had to smile in spite of everything, thinking if only Gen. Howard could see him now. He hoped Laura Yoder wasn't there to witness his disgrace.

"What's so funny?" Young Ticknor asked.

"Nothing," Morgan said. "It's kind of funny, that's all."

"I don't see nothing funny about it. I'd have killed that fat fucker if you hadn't hit him first."

Morgan was feeling the side of his head. It had a nice throb to it. It was beginning to swell, but that was normal. "No call for any killing. Lattimer is just a drunk fool. The man was unarmed. You'd be facing the rope if you'd killed him."

The kid handed Morgan his hat. "Just the same, it wasn't right what he did."

Morgan sleeved dirt from his hat and put it on. "Of course it wasn't right, but you can't kill every fool that crosses your path. There wouldn't be a cemetery big enough to hold them. You're too ready with that gun, kid.

Save it for the important killing, if that should be necessary in the course of our travels.''

Morgan went over to where Lattimer was propped against the wall of the saloon. "How is he?" he asked. "I hit him pretty hard."

"He'll live," one of the men said. "You know, Henry isn't a bad sort when he doesn't have the drink in him."

Morgan just nodded and walked away with the kid trailing after him. "What'd you want to do that for, Mr. Morgan. Asking after the health of a man like that?"

Morgan didn't slacken his pace. "I wanted to be sure he wasn't going to die of a cracked skull. We'd have the law coming after us if he did that, which is something we don't need. Stop harping on it, we've got business to attend to."

Down in the Pool, the local name for the city docks, passengers were coming off a steamer that had just docked. Most of them were men. Some of them could be Halliday gunmen brought up the coast from San Francisco. There were plenty of gunmen for hire on the Barbary Coast. It could be more of Laura Yoder's fanciful bullshit, but he would pass on the information, for what it was worth, to Gen. Howard. What the general planned to do with any such information he had no way of knowing.

On the way to the stable they stopped to listen to a shouter at an open air meeting. A daytime meeting was strange in itself. Usually they held them at night, with torchlight and drums. There was no speaker's platform. They were using the porch of a small hotel that fronted on the main street.

The shouter was a man about 40, with wild eyes to go with his mane of thick, wild hair. Morgan thought he recognized him as a tinhorn politician who had once stopped off at Spade Bit looking for votes. Territorial representative, something like that. Now he was cursing and damn-

48

ing the Indians, calling them red niggers, demanding that they be removed from the territory, exterminated if they refused to go. He had no particular tribe in mind. All Indians were red-nigger murderous bastards, a cancer on society, an obstacle to progress, and would have to go or be wiped out.

"We must show no mercy," he shouted, "for they will show no mercy to us. If we don't move against them now, it will be too late. Those of you who were here at the time of the old war know what I'm talking about. Before the army made it too hot for Joseph, the treacherous red bastard, and he tried to escape to Canada, his savages butchered and raped and burned up and down this territory. I lost my family to these pox-ridden, dog-eating degenerate beasts. They raped my wife and daughter, mutilated their privates, then killed them and scalped them. And they'll do it again, do it to your womenfolk, if we don't stop them before they get started."

The shouter paused for a drink of water. "Gen. Phil Sheridan had it right, my friends. 'The only good Indian is a dead Indian,' is what he said, and never a truer word was spoken. And, mind you, Phil Sheridan wasn't just saying the popular thing, wasn't looking for votes. He fought the Indians long and hard, witnessed their atrocities at first hand, and he hated the bastards. Wipe them out, he recommended, no more peace parlays, no more treaties, cleanse the earth of their filthy presence. . . . "

"Come on," Morgan said to the kid. "Enough bullshit for one day.

"But it wasn't all bullshit, Mr. Morgan."

"No, it wasn't. Chief Joseph's warriors did all those things. And our people, the militia, did the same to them. It was a dirty, vicious war. We pushed Joseph too hard and he struck back. Indians have no notion of civilized warfare, if there is such a thing. They torture, they rape, they kill old people and children. It could happen again like the man said. What's different now is Halliday is trying to make it happen. An Indian uprising would give him all the excuse he needs. Crush the uprising, kill as many Indians as he can, round up the others, ship them off to Oklahoma. Trouble is, it may not be that easy. If the Indians get into wild country, it would be hell to flush them out. They could raid and kill like Joseph did before he ran for Canada.''

Morgan was walking fast, wanting to get out of this town, but the long-legged kid had no trouble keeping up with him. "You don't like Injuns, do you, Mr. Morgan?''

Morgan wanted to choke off this conversation. It was bringing back bad memories of the old war. He remembered a bitter cold morning when they trapped a breakaway band of Joseph's warriors in a dead-end canyon, a narrow place with sheer rock walls and no way out the other end. The Indians wouldn't give up so they killed them all with heavy rifle fire and a light mountain gun. It didn't take much to kill them: they were half dead with hunger. Back at Spade Bit Gen. Howard had asked him if he remembered the blood on the snow. He remembered it all right.

"I'm not sentimental about Indians," Morgan said. "Some of them are vicious sons of bitches, just like our own people. If war comes, for whatever reason, they'll have to be put down. The territory has come too far to turn back. Come on now. Let's not be dwelling on the rights and wrongs of this. We have work to do.''

Young Ticknor remained silent while they saddled their horses, loaded up the pack animal, and headed for the bridge that spanned the Snake at the end of town. If they didn't cross the Snake here, they would have a hell of a time crossing it south of Lewiston. It was a wild river and had to be treated with respect. The man who fooled with it could easily lose his life, like so many others.

They were heading for the deep woods just north of

the Salmon River. Father Boudreau's mission Indians operated a sawmill there, shipping out the finished boards several times a year, part of the priest's effort to give the Indians some self respect and to make some money at the same time. Morgan knew this from the newspapers his top hand, Sid Sefton, read from cover to cover. Sid had learned to read and write late in life and couldn't get enough of the printed word. What he read, he liked to pass on, even if it made you yawn. Ask him to name all the petty politicians in some remote county and he could do it. Morgan knew about Father Boudreau and his mission because of Sid.

It was wild country surrounding the mission. The Salmon was as wild a river as there was in Idaho. They called it the River of No Return with good reason, so many men had been lost in the gorges and canyons it flowed through. Mountains hemmed it in for a good part of its length, one peak higher than the other, and it flowed so fast that long stretches of it were thick with foam. Some of the mountains had never been explored or even penetrated by man—white or Indian. A man or a party of men could disappear in there and not leave a trace.

Morgan was thinking about that as they rode south from Lewiston. It would take a day's ride to get to where the Salmon flowed into the Snake. When they reached the joining of the rivers, they would follow the Salmon east as best they could. There were rough roads north of the river. Some of them went nowhere but to long abandoned mines or lumber camps in the mountains. They would stay with the river as much as possible. At least it was coming from where they wanted to go.

It was a warm day. The country around Lewiston was the lowest point in the territory and so the weather was mild for most of the year. Morgan took off his lined coat and laid it on the saddle in front of him. He didn't think they were riding into a trap. That would be too elaborate

51

when a bushwhacker's bullet would do just as well. But there could be something going on in there. No better place for sneaky doings. Which brought him back to the question: why would Halliday's agents be handing out guns to Indians so far back in the wilderness? There were a few isolated mines in that country, but nothing owned by the big companies. It was a puzzlement all right.

Morgan didn't like puzzles, didn't like playing detective. He was no good at it, was too impatient. He liked to take things head-on and to hell with the consequences. That wasn't possible here and now. He had to wander the country with this kid, spinning this horsecock yarn about looking for new stock. He was stuck with it and stuck in it and it made him mad. He should have told the general to go hire himself a Pinkerton. The thought made him smile in spite of his sour mood. He didn't know why he felt so sour. Usually he took things as they came. Maybe it was because his head hurt and a fierce headache was starting up.

The sun was going down and they still had a long way to go before they reached the Salmon River.

"You're awful quiet, Mr. Morgan," the kid said.

Morgan glared at him. "Do me a favor, will you. Don't talk. For the love of Jesus, don't talk. I don't want to talk and I don't want to listen. You get that."

"Sure thing, Mr. Morgan," the kid said, "but before I stop talking there's something you should know."

"What is it?" Morgan said wearily.

"There's a dozen bottles of beer loaded on the pack horse. I bought them while you were busy with Miss Yoder. I know how you like your beer. Sundays you always sit on the porch and drink beer. A lot of beer, and you don't even get wild."

Morgan shook his head and the slight movement brought pain. "Are you making me out to be a drunkard, young fella?"

"Not one bit, Mr. Morgan." The kid sounded sincere. "I know how you like your beer and would prob'ly forget to pack any for the long ride. That's all I was thinking when I bought the beer."

"You did good." Morgan meant it. "We'll make camp before it gets too dark. My goddamned head hurts more than I thought it would. Be good to get into my blankets."

The kid was pleased to be praised. "You just turn in and I'll cook supper and uncap a couple of bottles of beer."

"A better idea," Morgan told him. "Why don't you uncap a couple right now."

Morgan drank cool beer as he rode. It wasn't San Francisco steam beer, but it was cool and wet and it eased the pain in his head.

The kid was turning out a lot better than he expected.

Chapter Five

Two more bottles of strong beer, drunk with his supper, sent Morgan into a deep sleep that cured his godawful headache.

It was gone when he opened his eyes at first light, and so was his sour mood. His face and the side of his head were sore to the touch. Otherwise, he was all right. Thinking back on it, he wondered if the fight could have been avoided if he'd drunk beer with Lattimer, tried to jolly him along. He didn't think so. Lattimer was spoiling for a fight and would not be denied. Anyway, you could only go so far toward keeping the peace. Past that point you'd lose respect for yourself.

He was glad the kid had been there. If he hadn't, he might have taken a bad beating from Lattimer and his friends. He could have shot them, of course, or held them off with his gun, but he wasn't sure drawing his gun would have stopped them. Once his gun was out, it could have come to killing and that would have brought the law down on top of him. At least that had been avoided, thanks to the kid.

Young Ticknor knew he was awake, but didn't say anything. He was at the fire cooking breakfast. The bacon and coffee smelled good to Morgan, who hadn't eaten that much the night before. They had made camp on a hill near the place where the Salmon joined the Snake. The subdued roar of the two turbulent rivers came from down below.

Morgan got out of his blankets and the kid said, "I already seen to the animals, Mr. Morgan. Watered and grained them and now they're eating grass over yonder. See."

The three horses, on long tethers, were grazing along the side of the hill, where the grass was thick. It was a mild, damp morning. It had rained during the night and there were thin patches of fog that would burn off as soon as the sun was full up.

They were on their way while the light was still grey. They had about 90 miles to go, but if they started early and camped late, they could make it in three days. If we're lucky, Morgan thought. Naturally they would find the mission sooner or later, but Morgan didn't want to spend too much time on this in case the whole thing turned out to be nothing at all. They were going far from the settled areas, the towns and villages where the war talk was. The war, just talk for now, could be burning up the territory by the time they got back.

A rough road, more like a track, followed the river. If anybody used it, there was little sign of it. There were wagon tracks, mostly washed away by rain, but it was heading in the right direction. In one place it had crumbled away and fallen into the gorge of the river. Here they had to dismount and lead the horses. They got the pack horse across first. If the pack horse didn't make it, they'd be without food and coffee. They could do without the coffee, but trying to shoot their meat in this bleak country would waste a lot of time. And Morgan was very mindful of the remaining eight bottles of beer. He had decided to ration himself to one bottle a day, to be drunk after they made camp. It would be something to look forward to.

Their luck held and on the morning of the third day Morgan figured they must be getting close. The mission was to the north of the river. that was all they knew for the moment. There was a long stretch where the road gave out and they had to travel over bare rock. The rock was smooth and there was a drop to one side of it. Here they had to lead the horses for nearly a mile. There were wagon tracks on the rock, faint but recognizable, and whoever had taken a wagon through here was one hell of a driver.

After the rock gave out and they mounted up again, Young Ticknor made a good point. "Looks like that priest has gone to a lot of trouble to hide his mission up here. Not much temptation for his Injuns, this neck of the woods."

Morgan had been thinking the same thing. The whiskey peddlers who made their way in here would have to be the most determined men in the world. Unless there was another way in than the one they were taking now. For the first hundred miles of its length, after it left its source in the Sawtooth Range, the Salmon flowed through flat country dotted with lakes. But that country was way off to the eastern end of the territory. A road could come through there. Morgan just didn't know.

He knew Father Boudreau couldn't hide an entire mission. What he was trying to do, it looked like, was keep his Indians out of harm's way. Morgan seemed to remember that the priest had his mission in a more populated area before he moved his Indians to the Salmon River country. Probably had trouble where he was to begin with, and that would figure. Indians running a sawmill would not be a popular idea where there were sawmills operated by whites.

"Hey, there's a track leading off here," Young Ticknor said, pointing.

It was a track sure enough and it ran up a hill and through a stand of pines. They got to the top of the hill and the track went on before them. The downside of the hill was a long slope with pines growing in close to the track. The track seemed to go straight to a small mountain with taller mountains stacked behind it. Morgan hoped they wouldn't have to go that far, but there was no way to tell. There was no sign of the mission or anything else. No woodsmoke, no buzzing of a sawmill, no hammering or planing, none of the workaday sounds that would carry far in the great silence of this lost country. The sun was hot and there wasn't even a breeze stirring the branches of the trees.

"We might as well go ahead," Morgan said.

"Might as well," the kid said. "We've come this far. You know, if they're in there, they're keeping mighty quiet about it. Is it Sunday?"

"It's not Sunday. Let's go."

Morgan knew this was where the mission was. He could not have explained how he knew. No believer in hunches or the sixth sense or any of that bull, the feeling was strong just the same. And there was the feeling of danger.

They walked their horses down the slope and into the trees at the bottom. For a while the track was in shadow, the trees growing in close. After the trees cleared a bit, they saw buzzards planing down low in the distance. The buzzards planed and banked and then disappeared as they dropped down.

"They're going after something dead or the garbage has just been put out." Young Ticknor shaded his eyes with his hat. "What do you think, Mr. Morgan?"

"It's one or the other." Morgan knew the kid was right, it couldn't be anything else.

When they got to the top of another hill they saw the mission. It looked more like a Nez Perce village than a mission. A few squat buildings looked like what you'd find in a white man's town. They were built of logs and Morgan figured one was the sawmill because it was open at both ends. He reached down to his saddlebag and found a small pair of brass-framed binoculars. They were old and he'd had them for years. There wasn't much call for them on the ranch. The lenses were dirty and he gave them a quick rub with his bandanna before he could see anything.

That was the sawmill, all right. He could make out the great shining blade of the saw. One of the other buildings was a planing shed. It was open at both ends like the sawmill and there were tall stacks of boards beside it. The third building in the white man's style was probably a schoolhouse. As he moved the glasses he saw a very small house set back from the mission village, barely visible through the trees. That would be the priest's house, small, modest, painted white. It was as if the priest didn't want to intrude on the Nez Perce village. The priest must have been a kind and generous man, had let them have their way, hadn't tried to make them into what they were not.

Morgan moved the binoculars back and forth. The village was deserted, there was no one there. Nothing moved, not even a dog. The Indian houses, set in a wide circle, were intact, but empty.

Morgan handed the binoculars to Young Ticknor. "There's nobody down there. Look for yourself."

Young Ticknor took his time. "They're gone someplace. You think they could be watching us, laying back in those trees?"

Morgan put the binoculars away. "I doubt it. You didn't see any dogs, did you."

"You're right. Your would expect to see dogs. But where's the priest? He's the boss man, after all. So where is he?"

"Where is everybody? Listen, I'm going down there to take a look. I want you to circle out wide and try to find what those buzzards are after. It could be just a dead animal, but try to find it so we'll know. Take it slow so you don't run into anything. The first sign of danger, fire a shot and I'll get to you fast. Be careful, you hear me?"

"I hear you."

The kid took his horse off the track and headed into the pines. In less than a minute there was no sign of him. Morgan walked his horse down into the village. If someone was there, and wanted to kill him, it wouldn't be that hard to do. It would be easy if they knew how to use a rifle. But nobody shot at him. There was no sound, no movement. The circle the Indian houses were built around was wide, dusty, bare, hard-packed by the passage of many feet over many years. Here and there were the blackened remains of cook fires, but the iron supports for cook pots and the pots themselves were gone.

Back of the houses horses, not many, had been kept. Rain had blurred their hoofprints so they had been gone for days. Morgan stopped looking in the deserted Indian houses after he got to the biggest, which must have been where the old chief, Notus, lived. It was as empty as the others.

The machinery in the sawmill building had not been removed. The steam engine that provided power for the saw was cold. The only place he hadn't checked was the priest's little house, standing back in the pines. He went there now. The kid hadn't come back yet.

The house had a small, narrow porch, and he stood on it listening for sounds. Something, more a movement than a sound, made him draw his gun. The door was open and he went in. It was a single story house: one room that doubled as sleeping quarters, a small built-on kitchen in back. A door in the kitchen closed softly. It had opened by itself before he got to it. But someone had been there: the airless little house smelled of woman. An Indian woman. He could smell the beargrease she used on her hair, the perfume Indian women made from roots and tree bark. He looked through the house, but it had been stripped of everything. None of what he saw made sense.

He was walking back through the village to wait for the kid when a woman appeared in the doorway of the chief's house. He would have missed her if she hadn't called to him. It was the middle of the afternoon, with bright sunshine, but she startled the hell out of him. He put his gun away and walked toward her. She was a very good-looking Indian woman, and she wasn't smiling. She was dressed in traditional Nez Perce clothing: beaded deerskin skirt, bright vest secured by leather thongs rather than buttons. She wore moccasins and had her jet black hair skinned back and tied behind her head. Her hair was thick with grease and she had eyes like black olives. She stood without moving, waiting for him to get close.

Morgan knew a few words of the Nez Perce language. He said, "Where is everybody?"

"Everybody is gone," she answered in English.

Morgan wasn't too surprised. She had learned English from the priest. "Gone where?"

"To the Colville reservation in Washington. Father Boudreau took them there. Soon there will be a war and he wanted them to have no part in it. The priest knows the Indian agent there and he will take them in. They left everything behind, as you see."

Morgan saw that she wore nothing under the vest. The skimpy garment did little to hide her large breasts. This could hardly have been her everyday dress, with a priest around. But maybe it was: Father had the reputation of being free and easy with his Indians. Just the same, there was something about her that wasn't right.

"Why are you still here?" he asked.

"When I left the reservation, I swore I would never go back. To that reservation or any other."

It was a straight enough answer, but what did it mean? What was she going to do, a woman alone, 90 miles or so from the closest town. An Indian woman, at that.

"But where will you go?" Morgan didn't give a fuck where she went, but her presence here puzzled him.

"Far from Idaho where they hate us so much. I can speak English. I can do something. Father Boudreau taught me bookkeeping. I can do that."

Not in that get-up, Morgan thought. And somehow he knew she had tricked herself out the way she was after the priest left. It was as if she had put on a costume. He didn't believe her horsecock about going far from Idaho. It had a nice dramatic ring to it, but it was phony.

A strong smell came from her, but it was not unpleasant. Far from it, it made his cock take notice. No matter what Father Boudreau hoped for, this was no tame Indian bookkeeper, eager to learn white ways, but a wild woman. Quiet spoken though she was right now, the savagery came off her with a primitive force of its own.

Morgan liked wild women, but he hesitated when she backed into the chief's house, beckoning him to follow her. Still, he went in after her, horny old bastard that he was. The kid was out there somewhere, but Morgan wasn't too concerned about him. A man that fast with a gun could look after himself.

There was some sort of mystery surrounding this woman that Morgan felt he had to penetrate or the long trip would have been for nothing. And he wanted to penetrate her. They called them red Indians, but that was wrong most of the time. This good looking woman's skin was a sort of golden brown, healthy and rich, shining with the oil she had rubbed on it. Under the long skirt that nearly touched the ground, he knew her golden thighs would be strong and vigorous. What he was thinking was madness, but he couldn't help it. He couldn't help but think of her as some kind of enemy, dangerous as hell, and he didn't care. It was like a dream, finding a woman like this in a deserted mission, and still he didn't care. In this strange place she aroused him so much that he was ready to rape the ass off her. Brutal rancher attacks innocent Indian maiden. He didn't think it would come to that.

Why she wanted to fuck him was not easily explained. As with the lady reporter, maybe she just wanted to be hosed, though there was no reason why she should have gone without cock. Even at a mission there must have been plenty of young Indian lads who wanted to give her the micky. And who could resist her. However it went, Morgan had no such intention. Under the circumstances, fucking her was without a doubt the wrong thing to do. Detective work, he tried to convince himself, this is part of my investigation.

There was nothing to lie down on but the bare earth. That would do fine. The old chief's house was clean and the only smell was wood-smoke. She did no talking after she beckoned him into the light wood and rawhide house. He didn't think she was planning to kill him. If she did, she would have to do it with her bare hands. There was no war hatchet in sight, no knife. All Morgan knew was this: he'd fuck her first and ask more questions later. He knew his old friend, Police Chief Nathan Bender of Kansas City, formerly a detective lieutenant, would not approve of his methods, but what did Bender know of life on the frontier?

She lay down on the bare earth and Morgan lay down beside her. He didn't know her name and as far as he could tell she didn't know his. It was best to leave things as they were. Best not to know her name if he had to shoot her.

Not wanting to be shot himself, he put his gun well out of her reach when he unbuckled his gunbelt. They didn't take off their clothes, not all the way. Morgan got her skirt and vest unfastened and she lay half naked and golden brown. Her cunt hair was as shiny black as the hair on her head. A good smell came from her cunt when she opened her legs. Morgan knew she was ready when he saw a little trickle of warm fuck juice leaking from her cunt lips.

He took off his coat and shirt, but not his pants. Anything could happen here, though he had no idea what it might be, and he didn't want to be struggling into his pants when he should be trying to defend himself. He didn't take off his boots for the same reason. What he did was unbutton his pants and pull them down along with his underpants. It was a most ungallant way to fuck a lady, even an Indian lady, but better safe than sorry.

She didn't seem to mind any of it. She was waiting for him to plow into her. He got between her golden thighs and she gave his cock a few strokes before she guided it into her. She had rubbed her hands in her hair and they were oily when she stroked him. She stroked him so well with her oily hand that he nearly came all over her belly, but she knew that. He gave his cock a hard squeeze to stop him from shooting his load. It hurt his cock a little, and his balls sort of tightened up, but he didn't spoil it by wetting her belly with come.

She guided the head of his cock into her cunt and after that it was up to him. Lord, it felt good. Her lovely rounded golden ass was on the bare earth and she couldn't roll around. Sometimes that was all right, but right now he wanted her firmly in place. She was strong and was able to bounce her ass on the bare floor in spite of his weight on top of her. She did none of the cunt tightening white women did. She took the full length of his hot, thick cock as if she couldn't get enough of it. Morgan had a long one, a thick one, and she wanted more than he could give her. He tried, driving it right in to the hilt. She had her middle finger in his asshole and was making him crazy the way she used it, tickling and pushing the finger like a little cock. Not many women did that, and he liked it fine. He liked women who let themselves go, for what good was fucking if you didn't loosen up and do what was natural and enjoyable. Most people didn't know how to do that.

She fucked him without making a sound, silent but with fierce energy, her black eyes staring into his. Morgan wasn't used to women like that. White women usually gasped or grunted, shouted dirty words, and sometimes they screamed. This one did none of that, but he knew she was building up to what he thought of as a ferocious, savage orgasm. Her lovely golden body grew rigid and her hands dug into his flesh. Then she went into what seemed like an epileptic fit and she howled like a wolf. The sound was so otherworldly, the hair stood up on the back of Morgan's neck. He came into her and she was still writhing and howling under him after he was drained.

He was standing up, buttoning his pants, buckling on his gunbelt, when he heard the horses coming, the drumbeat of their hoofs on the baked earth of the village circle. And with that came the scream of war cries. He ran outside with his gun in his hand and saw four Indians on horseback, in full war paint, bearing down on him. An arrow whistled past his head and he shot the Indian who fired it off his fast moving pony. The dead man crashed to the ground and the riders coming along behind jumped their ponies over the body. The riderless pony, frightened by the gunfire, ran in circles.

Morgan fired at the other attackers as they swept past. He shot one of them in the back and the Indian tumbled off his pony with a scream. He fired at them until his gun was empty. He was reloading when they rode around the circle of houses and started to come back. He wished to hell he had his rifle, but it was with his horse tied to a tree out beyond the village. This time they rode straight at him, the arrows hissing in deadly showers. He killed another one, but then he saw more of the bastards coming through the trees. He knew he couldn't stay lucky even with the gun. There were too many of them. The Colt .45 held only six shots and he knew this time he wouldn't be able to reload before an arrow killed him.

They were coming at him full tilt. This time they meant to finish it. They were almost on top of him when he heard the crash of the kid's rifle. Morgan looked and saw him moving in from the direction of the priest's house. Every shot he fired, he killed an Indian. It was crazy the way he came out through the pines, firing steadily as he walked, cool and purposeful. Caught between Morgan and the kid, the Indians still alive tried to make a break for it. Morgan cut down two and the kid's deadly rifle brought the others down. The ponies ran away into the pines and suddenly it was quiet except for the cries of a wounded man. Before Morgan could stop him, the kid shot the Indian in the head.

The kid got to where Morgan was standing and he grinned. It was the last thing Morgan expected and it gave him a jolt. The kid had killed his first men, even if they were Indians, and he liked it. Morgan wondered if he'd be able to stop now that he'd had a taste of killing. He seemed to be mighty pleased with himself. Morgan didn't thank him. He didn't feel like thanking him though he had saved his life.

"You took a long time to get back," Morgan said.

Nothing could get at the kid in his moment of glory. "I found the priest's grave far back in the pines. He was buried shallow and the critters had dug him up. Eaten pretty bad, but it was the priest all right. Had his black gown on, or whatever they call it. Didn't have a shovel or nothing so I put him back in the hole and tried to find rocks to cover it. Looks like the wild ones killed him and chased off the others. What do you think, Mr. Morgan?"

The kid was completely calm. The death of the priest, the killing of the Indians, didn't even scratch the surface of his stony indifference. He might as well have been talking about a wagon with an axle that had to be replaced.

"I think it's a hell of a thing," was all Morgan could say.

Young Ticknor looked into the old chief's house. "Hey, there's a woman in there."

Morgan nodded. "So there is. And she's going to tell us what we want to know."

He was ready to kill her if she didn't.

Chapter Six

Morgan dragged her out in the open and told her to kneel. Then he put his pistol to her head and thumbed back the hammer. Her black eyes were defiant until she heard the sound of the hammer earing back. That brought a flicker of fear.

The dead Indians lay in the dust under a hot sun. It wouldn't be long before the bodies began to stink. The Indian woman, whatever her name was, didn't want to look at them. That was good, Morgan thought. The mission had civilized her enough to make her afraid of death.

With the muzzle of the pistol pressed to her head, Morgan said, ''My friend here found the priest's grave. Who killed him and why was it done? Where are the guns? What happened to the rest of your people? Answer my questions or I'll put a bullet in your brain. That is not just a threat, I'll do it.''

''Can I get up?''

"Stay as you are and start talking. Talk or die. That's the deal."

The kid stood to one side, staring at her, but saying nothing.

"Running Wolf killed the priest," she said. Sweat was running down her face, dripping from her chin. She looked nothing like the proud, savage Indian woman she wanted to be. Far from it—she was just a frightened woman who didn't want to die.

"Running Wolf hated the priest and wanted to kill him for a long time. He said the priest had stolen their manhood, turned them into tame Indians, men without balls. He cursed the priest and his sawmill and his prayers. The old chief went to the priest to warn him, but he just laughed. 'Running Wolf just didn't like to work, he said.' Running Wolf finally got up enough nerve to kill him."

Morgan held the .45 steady. "Was that after they brought in the guns?"

"Yes." Her voice was so low he could barely hear her. "Running Wolf said the guns would change everything. With the guns they could go far back into the mountains and live like men. Running Wolf said he got the guns from a man at one of Halliday's trading posts. I didn't understand it."

She looked at the dead Indians for the first time. "Running Wolf is over there."

Morgan ignored that, figuring Running Wolf must have been her cocksman. "But even if he hated the priest, why kill him? Why not go into the mountains with his followers and his guns?"

The woman licked her lips. "The priest found out about the guns. But that wasn't why Running Wolf killed him. He hated him because of what he had done to us. Can I have a drink of water?"

"Not yet," Morgan said. "Did you hate the priest? Did Running Wolf turn you against him?"

The grease from her hair was mixing with the sweat on her face. "Yes. I was his woman. He said we should have no gratitude or pity for the priest. If we were to become strong again, we must forget all the priest taught us. The priest had corrupted us and had to die. Killing him would be the first step toward getting back our true Indian nature."

Dreams of glory, Morgan thought. Dreams of bullshit. A good man who had devoted his life to these mission Indians was dead because of a crackpot who wanted to become another Geronimo. Or Crazy Horse, or somebody. Take your pick.

Morgan said, "Where are the guns? Why didn't they use them today?"

Kneeling in the hot sun, the woman looked ready to keel over. "They are in a cave far back in the mountains. There is food there and ammunition for the guns. You would not be alive now if they had the guns. But the guns are a day's ride from here."

There was regret in her voice and Morgan figured she was grieving for Running Wolf, the loony son of a bitch. He felt no pity for her. She was trying to lay off the murder of the priest on Running Wolf, but who was to say she hadn't been part of it. There wasn't mush else he wanted to know. After that she could weep over Running Wolf, bury the fucker if she could find something to dig with. He felt like shooting her, but knew he wouldn't.

"What happened to the old chief and the rest of your people?"

Still on her knees, her body began to sway with fatigue. "They became frightened after the priest was killed. The guns frightened them, too. They have gone to the Colville reservation in Washington. That is true."

That was enough. Morgan told her to get up. "We're going to leave you now. Find your own water. Catch a pony and ride out of here. I don't care what you do."

"But I have no food. I will die."

"Then die." Morgan turned away from her. "Come on, kid. Time we were getting back."

Riding away, Young Ticknor turned to look back. "She's still standing there. Lord, but you were tough with her. Would you have killed her if she hadn't talked?"

"I would. I'm not sure she didn't put Running Wolf up to this real Indian bullshit. I'm not sure she didn't kill the priest herself. I think she's an evil bitch."

They rode in silence for a while. Young Ticknor was thinking. "You don't hit it off too well with women, do you, Mr. Morgan? That Yoder lady. . . . "

"I was wrong about her. She was telling the truth."

Morgan was thinking Laura Yoder was too gutsy for her own good. They wouldn't hesitate to kill her if they discovered what she was up to. Neal would order it done and his thugs would see to it. All they had to do was weight her with chains and dump her in the Snake, never to be seen again.

He wondered what drove her to risk her life. It could hardly be concern for the Indians. She didn't strike him as a woman who cared much about other people of any color. Like as not, she hoped to make a big name for herself with the Halliday story. The Boise *Northwest Journal* was the best newspaper in the territory. But even a paper with a good reputation might not want to take on Halliday. All it would take was a can of kerosene and a match to put it out of business. An editor could get shot through his office window.

Young Ticknor said, "You know, I could have roped that Indian woman and taken her to General Howard."

"She'd change her story by the time you got to Boise. And even if she told a straight story, they wouldn't believe it. Drick Halliday handing out guns to the Indians, they'd never buy it. It would be a waste of time. She'd slow you up and be a danger to you."

The kid grinned at that. "A woman a danger to me?"

"You'll have to pass through some towns to get to Boise. With all this war talk, people would want to know what you were doing with an Indian woman. They could crowd you about it."

They were well clear of the mission by now. "They'd be sorry if they did," the kid said. "Dead sorry, if that's the way they wanted it."

Morgan looked at him, not liking the meanness he heard in the kid's voice. "I'm going to tell you one more time. Don't go killing people if you don't have to. Killing those Indians back there had to be done. I'm glad you were there to do it. I'd be dead if you hadn't showed up."

That was as close as Morgan came to saying thanks. The kid was full enough of himself as it was. Too much praise would swell his head beyond the size of his hat.

"Mr. Morgan," the kid said. "To me it was nothing at all. We work pretty good together, don't we?"

Kill pretty good together, was what he meant. Now that the kid had enjoyed his first taste of killing, he wouldn't be coming back to Spade Bit. That would be a mercy, but Morgan hoped to steer him away from life as a gunfighter. It would be a short life no matter how good he was. No deadlier gun than Hickok ever lived and he ended up shot in the back of the head by a smalltime gambler. But he wasn't the kid's father and he would have to make his own way in the world.

Three days later, they were back to where the two rivers met. The next morning they crossed the bridge across the Snake below Lewiston.

"I'll keep the pack horse," Morgan said. "Would just slow you up. Enough towns down along the Snake you can eat in. You might pick up some eatables for between towns. Follow the Snake down to Payette. There's a bridge there. Take the road that follows the Payette River to Montoun. The river branches off, but the road goes on to Boise. Gen. Howard is or will be at the Rathdrum Hotel. Like I said, wait for him if he isn't there.''

"You going to write out a report for him, Mr. Morgan?"

"No. You can tell him what's been happening. What Laura Yoder said about Halliday bringing gunmen in from San Francisco. What happened at the mission, all of it. Tell it to me as if you're talking to Gen. Howard."

Young Ticknor made a good report and Morgan thought it would do fine when he repeated it for the general. He still had no idea what Gen. Howard would do with the information. No doubt he'd be trying to call a meeting of people opposed to Halliday's plan for the removal of the Indians. They might come to such a meeting if they weren't too afraid of Halliday's thugs. If enough of them came, there wasn't much Halliday could do about it. His thugs couldn't crack the heads of several hundred people, especially if there were women in the crowd. What crowd? Morgan thought. The general would be lucky if he got a couple of dozen listeners.

The kid was ready to take off. "You figured out where we're going to hook up again?"

"Sort of. Halliday has a string of trading posts south of Craigment. Maybe four between Craigmont and Grangeville. His father had more, but there's less call for them now, so many new towns. Grangeville is where the biggest one is. Unless I have to move on, that's where I'll be. I'll meet you there in, say, two weeks from today."

"Whatever you say, Mr. Morgan. But what good will it do you scouting these trading posts. The Indian woman already told you the guns came from one of them. You can't go in there asking questions. Anyhow, what more is there to know?"

Morgan wanted the kid to be gone. "Maybe nothing. I want to take a look, that's all. Could turn up something.

Get going now. Grangeville, two weeks from today. You'll find the place.''

The kid turned his horse. "If you're there."

"I'll try to be there."

Morgan rode into Lewiston to see if he could find Laura Yoder. If she had anything more to tell him, all to the good. He couldn't just walk into the newspaper office and ask for her. Neal, the rat, would be immediately suspicious, and that would put her life in danger. Neal was one of Halliday's favorites, she'd said, and being so close to a powerful man had made him arrogant, thinking he couldn't be touched. Laura Yoder would be a dead woman if Neal had serious doubts about her.

Morgan didn't know where she lived and trying to find her boarding house would be a real chore and maybe dangerous for her. Lewiston was full of boarding houses, ratty and respectable, and for that matter, maybe she lived in a hotel. Plenty of hotels, too.

Once again, Morgan thought how ill-suited he was for this detective work. A professional detective would know how to find her without attracting too much attention. Morgan did not. Saying he was her cousin from. . . . Hell, he didn't even know where she came from originally. Bullshit like the long lost cousin wouldn't work. He'd have to figure out something else.

Morgan thought of the bartender at the fancy saloon beside the town hall where the lawyers hung out, a hearty, affable fellow who seemed to know everyone, had a good word for all his regular customers. There was a good chance he would know where Laura Yoder lived. Of course, he might not want to give that information to a stranger. Money might work if nothing else did. Best bet would be to let the bartender think he was interested in the lady. That would be easy to understand.

The place was half empty when Morgan got there. Two men who looked like lawyers were in a friendly argument about some court decision. "It's bad law no matter how you look at it," one of them was saying.

The bartender was leaning against the back shelves, reading a newspaper. He straightened up when Morgan stepped up to the bar. "What'll it be, mister?"

"Bottle of Frisco steam beer."

Morgan put a silver dollar on the bar. "Keep the change." It was all right to say that. There wasn't that much change; the bartender nodded thanks and turned to go back to his newspaper.

"Say," Morgan said, "maybe you recall I was in here about a week ago. Had a drink with Miss Laura Yoder from the newspaper."

"Sure. All she wanted was a short beer. You got it for her."

"Wish I had a memory like that."

"You got to have a good memory in this business. If you're looking to find her, why don't you try the newspaper? If she's not there, I don't know what to say. She hasn't been in here since she had that drink with you. Which is strange. Usually she comes in at least once a day, has her short beer, talks to the lawyers and so forth. A real go-getter, that gal."

Morgan didn't know what to think. A reporter with a fixed routine for gathering news wouldn't change it just like that. The town hall crowd, politicians and lawyers, would be the best source of news in Lewiston, and she wouldn't stop quizzing them for no reason. Of course, she could be down with the flu, something like that, but he didn't think so. It gave him a bad feeling.

"Maybe she's sick," he said to the bartender. "You wouldn't happen to know where she lives, by any chance. I'd like to look in on her, talk to her about the horse she's thinking of buying. I'm in the horse business north of here and I'll be going home today. She's a nice gal and I'll sell her a good horse at a good price."

The bartender laughed. "Guess she's tired of that old buggy she's been getting around in. Let me think a minute. Sure. She lives at Mrs. Flagler's boarding house—ladies only—up on Major Andrew Henry Street. It's a short street cut into the side of the hill, right up from Main Street. Just past the bank, make a left turn, there it is. But you could save time by asking after her at the paper."

"I'll do that." Morgan drank the last of his beer.

"If you see her, tell her we've been missing her. If she's sick, tell her to get well. This old place ain't the same without her."

Morgan thanked the man and went looking for Mrs. Flagler's boarding house. Major Andrew Henry Street was short and narrow, dug out of the side of a hill, with all the houses jammed together. Lewiston was short on building space and Morgan had seen other streets like this one.

He found a tall, new, white house with Mrs. Flagler's name over the door. Under it was a sign: REFINED YOUNG LADIES ONLY. Beside the door was a bell that rang if you turned a knob. A servant girl with a plain grey dress and a white cap came to the door.

"Didn't you see the sign, sir? Ladies only." She had an Irish accent.

With the door open, the house smelled of furniture wax. "I wasn't looking for a room. I'd like to see Miss Yoder, if she's at home. She's a friend of mine."

The maid gave Morgan a strange look and didn't seem to know what to say. A querulous voice, an elderly woman's voice, called out, "What is it, Bridget? Who is that out there?"

"A gentleman asking after Miss Yoder, Mrs. Flagler."

Mrs. Flagler, sixtyish and stern, came to the door and told the maid to get on with her work. Mrs. Flagler had a white mask of a face, but Morgan could see she was nervous.

"Miss Yoder isn't here," she said.

"Then where is she? I have to talk some business with her. Legitimate business."

"I told you she isn't here."

"And I asked you where she was."

Mrs. Flagler tried to close the door, but Morgan stopped it with his boot. Mrs. Flagler wasn't just nervous, she was very much afraid of something.

"Please go away, sir. I don't know where Miss Yoder is. She must have left town unexpectedly. Reporters go all over."

Morgan hoped the old lady wouldn't start yelling for help. She didn't, but her mouth trembled.

"I'm not leaving until you tell me where Laura Yoder is. I mean it. If something bad has happened to her, I want to know about it. I'll go to the law if I have to."

"The law!" The old lady's mouth twisted with contempt. "A lot of good that will do you, whoever you are."

"My name is Morgan. I have a horse ranch north of here."

"Maybe you do." Mrs. Flagler was showing some spirit. "You'd better come in."

Morgan followed her into a parlor full of overstuffed furniture. The picture over the mantelpiece was probably Mr. Flagler when he was alive. Mrs. Flagler had all the signs of widowhood. She pointed Morgan to a chair that looked as if it never had been sat on.

Mrs. Flagler sat on the edge of another chair. "You could be one of them for all I know. But I don't care. I'm afraid and I'm tired of being afraid. Miss Yoder left here six days ago. About nine o'clock, Sunday evening. Two men came to call on her and she left with them after a few minutes."

"Did she look as if they'd threatened her?"

"I can't say that she did. I just don't know. They waited in the parlor—right here—while I called her down from her room. Very little was said, and then they left. I didn't think very much about it. Miss Yoder kept some odd hours and, besides, one of the men delivers the *News* here in town and other towns closeby. His name is Oscar Newbold. Everybody knows him. Great big redheaded brute. The man with him had on a shabby suit and a funny looking hat. And he had a droopy mustache.''

"Did Miss Yoder take anything with her?"

"I told you she walked out of the house with Newbold and the other man. She didn't go back to her room. Do you think something bad has happened to her? When she didn't come back that night, I went to the newspaper the next morning. They said they hadn't seen her. Mr. Neal made a joke out of it, he suggested maybe she was stopping over with a gentleman friend. I waited until afternoon before I went to the chief of police. He said Miss Yoder was known to be a willful young lady and could be anywhere. He said he would make inquiries. I haven't heard from him since. That's all I can tell you."

Laura Yoder was probably dead, Morgan thought. Fuck the probably; she was dead. They wouldn't just run her out of town. She carried too much information in her head. It was hard to think of her dead. She'd been such a spirited woman, tough and hard, but honest. She seemed to take a lot of pride in her job, one of the few woman reporters in a rough business dominated by men.

"Did you tell the chief of police about Newbold and the other man?"

Mrs. Flagler's lip trembled. "Of course I did. Chief Potter said Mr. Neal, the editor, probably sent Newbold to fetch her to the office on some newspaper business. Newbold does all sorts of odd jobs when he isn't delivering the papers. The Chief said the other man was no doubt a drinking chum of Newbold's. He said they probably headed for a saloon after they escorted Miss Yoder to the office. Newbold is a big drinker."

Laura Yoder must have disappeared not long after she

left the house. It didn't take a detective to figure that. The way Morgan saw it, they walked her out of the house, telling her they had concealed guns ready to kill her if she balked. It was night and they could have walked her down to a dark part of the docks. They might not have bothered with a chain to sink her deep.

"You don't know if the chief ever talked to Neal, Newbold, or the other man?"

The old lady looked angry for a moment. "I don't know what he did. He said he would make inquiries and that's all he said. To say it plainly, he didn't seem too interested. I haven't gone back to him because I don't think it would do any good. He is a lazy crook, if you ask me. But for God's sake don't tell him I said that. I have to live in this town."

"And you haven't talked to Neal since that first time?"

"That's right. I'm afraid of him."

There it was, Morgan thought. They had murdered a woman and nothing was being done about it. Neal must have caught her eavesdropping or going through his papers late at night. Whatever it was, it was enough to mark her for death. The chief was in Neal's pocket and Neal was in Halliday's pocket. A nice arrangement. Morgan felt a dull rage beating in his head. By Christ, he'd do something about it. Killing Yoder's killers was not what he had set out to do, but he was going to do it just the same. His so-called detective work would have to wait.

He had a final question for Mrs. Flagler. "Did Newbold come back here and threaten you to keep quiet? Did anybody?"

The old lady shook her head. "Nobody. I'm an old lady and I guess they thought they had nothing to fear from me. They're right, in a way. I'm still afraid, so much so I can't sleep. But I've told you what I know, so I guess I'm not so fearful after all. I hope it won't get me into terrible trouble."

Morgan stood up. "You never talked to me. You can depend on that."

The old lady got up to see Morgan out. At the door, she grasped his hand and a single tear ran down her chalky white face. "Mr. Morgan, I hope you can do something. Miss Yoder was a nice young woman and it isn't right something like this should happen to her."

"I'll do something about it," Morgan said. "You can depend on that."

Walking away from the house, he thought it was strange the way things turned out. At the time when he was worrying about what might happen to Laura Yoder she was already dead. He had no ironclad proof that she was dead, but he didn't need it. He was as sure she was dead as if he could see her laid out in her coffin.

As the old lady said, it wasn't right that something like this should happen to her. It was a mild remark, but it summed it up just right. It said it better than any number of loud cries for vengeance. The men who killed her, the man who sent them to kill her, had to be killed themselves. Nothing else would do.

It was still light. He would have to wait till dark. Meanwhile, he could look for Oscar Newbold in the saloons.

Chapter Seven

Morgan thought there was a good chance that Newbold did his drinking in the saloon in the same block as the newspaper office. He had seen it on the first day he and the kid had come to Lewiston. Men in ink-stained aprons were going in or coming out. They had the look of men sneaking a quick beer while the boss's back was turned. Typesetters, printers, men who worked for Halliday's paper.

Newbold didn't have to be a regular drinker there. He might owe too much on the slate, he could be barred from the place for fighting or other bad behavior. He didn't have to be there at this time of day, though there was a good chance he was. It was after six o'clock and the day shift would have left the newspaper building by now.

Morgan went in and stood at the bar drinking a beer. There was a mixed crowd, a good deal of noise. He could tell the newspaper workers from the others by the paper hats some of them wore. Mrs. Flagler had described Newbold as a great big redheaded brute. None of the drinkers fitted the description. Morgan paid for another beer and decided to wait.

He couldn't ask questions. Did Newbold drink there? What time did he come in? Somebody would remember that when Newbold turned up missing, and Newbold would disappear. So would his pal if he could nail down his identity. He wanted to put them in the river where he was sure they had put Laura Yoder. That was his plan but he would change it if necessary. He would kill them wherever he found them, if that's how it had to be. All things considered, the river was the best way to get rid of them. Once they were dead, the swift current would take them far from Lewiston.

He didn't want the law after him so he would try not to use his gun. But he would if he had to. Gunshots in the night were not uncommon in a tough town like Lewiston, and maybe he'd get away with it. It wouldn't be so easy, though, to go after Neal if he had to shoot Newbold and his friend. As soon as the bodies were discovered, and Neal knew about it, he would run for cover. And that, Morgan thought, would be no good at all.

He knew Gen. Howard would not approve, far from it. He would tell him to put his trust in the law. If the law in Lewiston is corrupt, go to the territorial police and tell them your story. That and a nickel—as the old joke had it—would get you a five-cent beer.

He didn't turn to look when Oscar Newbold and another man came in. Instead, he watched them in the mirror behind the bar. It had to be Newbold. He was a huge man with his red hair clipped short. He drove a delivery wagon so he didn't wear a paper hat like the men in the pressroom. His hat was a gray derby and he wore it on the back of his head. He wore Levi pants with the bottoms turned up and a thick red woolen shirt. The man with him was dressed in a town suit, ill-fitting and rumpled. His hat was a grey fedora, as battered as his suit, with a high crown, a wide band, and a narrow brim. He had a soup-strainer mustache that gave him a doleful look. He was as Mrs. Flager had described him.

Morgan bought another beer. It looked like Newbold was right popular with the other drinkers. It was Oscar this, and Oscar that. How's the world treating you, Oscar? Getting much, Oscar? When're you going to run for mayor, Oscar?'' Shit like that.

Morgan could see that Newbold was already half drunk. "My fellow Americans," he bellowed when the joking trailed off. "I am prepared to stand one round of drinks and that has to be it. We've had a fine time all week, but now my money is running low."

That brought expressions of sympathy and one man said, "You spent it when you had it, Oscar. Nobody can fault you in that department."

"Thank you, Mr. Fitzpatrick." Newbold had a voice like a bull. He was playing the bluff, hearty good fellow, but his little green eyes gave him away. No matter how much he roared or back-slapped, his deepset eyes darted this way and that, suspicious and watchful.

There is one mean, vicious bastard, Morgan thought. It was hard to figure his friend. From his looks he could be a clerk in a fleabag hotel, an undertaker's assistant, or a salesman with a line of shoddy goods. He had been drinking, but wasn't drunk.

"Now if you good people will step up to the bar. . . . " Newbold put some silver dollars on the bar, then he rooted through his pockets looking for more money. Finally he got to his back pocket and pulled out two twenties. "By Gorry, there's life in the old boy yet."

The silver dollars and part of a twenty paid for the round of drinks. After that, Newbold and his friend found a table and drank by themselves. Newbold drank whiskey with beer chasers, his friend nothing but beer, but he drank a lot of it. Morgan stayed where he was at the bar. When the bartender put a beer in front of him, saying it was on good old Oscar, he drank it.

Nobody took any notice of him. There were a few stockmen and ranch hands there. By now it was dark outside and after a while it started to rain. That was all to the good, Morgan thought, it would keep people off the streets. Darkness and heavy rain were just what he needed.

It was getting late, 11:45, and the crowd of drinkers was thinning out. Men were turning up their coat collars, getting ready to brave the heavy rain that hadn't let up for hours. Newbold and his pal were still at their table, still drinking. It looked like he was going to be left with the two men he wanted to kill. That was no good, so he finished his beer and went out into the rain to wait for them.

He had to stand in a doorway for most of an hour before they finally came out of the saloon. Newbold was very drunk and singing as loud as he could. The other man wasn't doing anything but walking unsteadily beside Newbold. They passed Morgan without seeing him. He let them get a little way ahead before he started to follow them. Even if they had looked back, they might not have seen him, the rain was so heavy. There was no one else on the street.

Morgan was close enough to hear what Newbold was going on about after he quit singing. He called the other man Sully. "My dear friend, Sully," he said, needlessly shouting in the quiet street, "we've had a corker of a week and don't you be denying it. All the booze we could drink, all the cunt we could fuck. It was a nice clean job and we got well paid for it."

Morgan had to strain to hear what Sully was saying. It sounded like, "Not so loud, for Christ's sake. You want to get us nailed?"

Newbold was in too good a mood to be put off by that. "Don't be so nervous, you nervous little bugger. We're home free, I'm telling you. We couldn't be more in the clear. I just wish we had a money job to carry us through next week."

Morgan heard the fear in Sully's voice. "I'm going to walk away from you, you keep on like this. I mean it, Oscar."

"Wait! Wait! I got to take a piss." Newbold unbuttoned his pants and pissed against the side of a building. "Got to water the horse, old man. I cannot understand how you can swallow so much beer and not piss more than you do. Ah, that feels good. Nothing like a good piss, I always say."

Sully said irritably, "Don't be such a horse's ass, Oscar. Can't we hurry it up a bit. I'm soaked to the skin."

Newbold wheeled around and caught Sully by the throat. "How can you call me a horse's ass and me your brother-in-law. True, your sister is dead, but you're still my brother-in-law. Who gave you a place to stay after you got out of the pen? Who put you in the way of making some easy money? Me, that's who. So quit your bellyaching and cheer up. We did a nice job, made some money, and we'll make some more. There's always work of that sort going round."

The docks were at the bottom of a slope that ran down from Main Street. It was paved with cobblestones that glistened in the rain. Here and there were gaslamps that didn't shed much light. The rain pelted down in a steady downpour. At the bottom of the slope, on the docks, ships were tied up. Some of the ships showed lights. Morgan knew there would be a night watch on all the ships.

Past the area where the ships were tied up, the docks were dark and deserted. No gaslamps there. Morgan was moving up behind the two men when a police wagon came clattering down the street. Prisoners in the paddy wagon were yelling in some foreign language. Sailors making a night of it. Morgan slowed his pace until the paddy wagon went by. Then he moved in again.

Sully yelped with fright when Morgan said, "I'll shoot you dead if you don't do as I say. You hear me, Newbold?"

Newbold swung around and nearly fell down doing it. Sully was shaking. "What the hell is going on here?" Newbold shouted. "Are you a robber or what?"

Morgan pointed the gun at Newbold's face. "That's what I am. Walk along ahead of me or get shot."

Newbold turned his back to Morgan, but didn't move. "For fuck's sake, all we have is a few dollars between us. Take it if you're that hard up. You were in the saloon. I saw you. What's this walk along bullshit?"

Morgan kept some distance between himself and the two men. Poke a man in the back with a gun and you risk having it taken away from you.

"Do what I tell you. I won't tell you again."

Morgan knew how unpredictable drunks could be. You never knew what they were going to do. Drunk or sober, Sully wasn't the type to take on a man with a gun. Newbold might try it because he was big and tough as well as stupid.

"Move or get shot. Your last chance to do it. We're going down by the river, nice and quiet there, no bluecoats. You have more money than you're saying, you lying fuck, and you're going to cough it up. Now move."

The standoff was broken by Sully, who was trying to get his nerves under control. "Come on, Oscar, he just wants the money."

Newbold moved ahead, but he wasn't afraid. "You'll be sorry you did this. You think you can rob me and get away with it."

That could be whiskey courage, Morgan thought. Some of it was. It wasn't true that a shock sobered people up in a hurry, even if they were very drunk. What a shock did was sharpen a drunk's wits. He might still be drunk, but a shock enabled him to think better. Newbold was like that now, and Morgan didn't want him to catch on that this wasn't just a robbery.

"Come after me all you like," Morgan said to him. "I'll be long gone from here."

Newbold cursed him, but kept moving.

Back of the buildings on Main Street was the closest thing Lewiston had to a public park. The only entrance was a wide alley between a bank and a hotel. They had leveled the top of the slope that went down to the river. There was a small bandstand and picnic tables. A stepped footpath, with a handrail for the elderly, went down to the drop that fell to the fast moving water. Morgan knew it was there because he'd once shared a picnic basket with a good looking young whore on her day off. This was years back, but the park was still there, with the same sign hung over the alley: JOHN McLOUGHLIN MEMORIAL PARK.

He walked the two men through the alley and into the park. The only light here was reflected from Main Street. In the half-dark, with the rain coming down so hard, it was difficult to see anything. He got them to the footpath and told them to walk on down. Newbold cursed him, but Sully wanted to stay on his good side, if possible. Sully went first, holding onto the handrail. Sully was light and quick and had no trouble getting down. Newbold, big and awkward, nearly fell twice on the wet grass. Morgan was right behind him.

At the bottom was a sort of terrace with a low stone wall no more than two-feet high facing the river. There was a drop of about ten-feet on the other side of the wall. Standing by the wall with his back turned, Newbold growled, "What now, robber? You can search my boots, but I won't drop my pants. You'll have to kill me first."

Morgan chopped him across the back of the neck with the barrel of the Colt and pushed him over the wall. Newbold was unconscious when he hit the water. He'd be dead in less than a minute.

"That was for Laura Yoder," Morgan said quietly.

He didn't mean to frighten Sully by saying it. He didn't mean to say it at all. But Sully yelped when he heard it and tried to run. Morgan grabbed him by the neck and sat him on the wall. Sully shit his pants while he was doing it.

"Ah Jesus Christ, please mister, don't kill me!" Sully was trembling all over, like a man with a fever. "It was Oscar killed the woman. Strangled her. I wanted no part of it, but he made me come along. I never killed anybody in my life, but Oscar said I knew he was going to kill the woman and he'd kill me if I didn't take apart in it. What could I do? Oscar strangled the woman and he made me take hold of her ankles before she went in the river. I swear I thought he was going to throw me in after her. You know I'm telling the truth. Please don't kill me. It isn't fair that you should kill me."

Morgan told him to be quiet. "Shut your mouth or I'll throw you over. Listen to me, you fucking, sneaking rat, I don't specially want to kill you. You don't have to tell me Oscar killed the woman. I know he did. Your don't have the nerve to kill a cockroach."

Sully started to say something and Morgan slapped him so hard he nearly went over the wall. Morgan grabbed him before he fell backwards into the river. Sully would go into the river, but not just yet.

Sully took Morgan's grabbing him back to safety as a good sign. He got a little nerve back, such as it was. This time when he talked, Morgan let him talk. Let him think he had a chance of staying alive.

"You let me go and you'll never see me again. I'm just a small time forger and counterfeiter, never a killer,

I swear it. I never should have teamed up with Oscar. I . . . I don't mean teamed up, nothing like that. I was dead broke, had no place to live when I got out of the pen. Oscar is, was, my brother-in-law and he offered me a place to stay. That was my mistake, taking his offer, yes, sir, a terrible mistake. I'm awful sorry about the woman, I could cry when I think of it. But I've learned my lesson, yes, sir. From now on I'm going to try to live a decent life."

Morgan had heard enough. Like the condemned man waiting for the hangman, Sully still thought he had some kind of chance. Morgan could have let him fall into the river, but he hadn't. So there was hope in Sully's voice. Morgan liked the part about learning his lesson and wanting to live a decent life from here on in.

"I ought to hand you over to the law." Enough, Morgan told himself. Either he thinks he's going to stay alive or he doesn't. Troweling on more bullshit wasn't going to help very much.

"I'm not afraid to go to the law," Sully said. "I'll explain to the court how Oscar threatened me. I did what I did for fear of my life. I was acting"—Sully searched for the word—"acting under duress."

The little fucker was a jailhouse lawyer. He figured he'd get off if he came to trial. No witnesses to the murder.

Morgan jolted him with, "Who told Oscar to kill the woman? Was it Neal, the editor? Answer up while you still have a chance."

Sully hedged a bit. "Oscar said it was Neal. I wasn't there. I've never been to the newspaper."

"You know who Drick Halliday is?"

"Yes. Sure I do."

"But you wouldn't know if Neal talked to Halliday about the woman and Halliday ordered her killed?"

"No! No! I don't know anything about that. Oscar told

me Neal told him to kill the woman. He didn't even tell me why she had to be killed. I asked him, but he wouldn't tell me. Oscar liked to hold things back. Honest to God, I'd tell you if I knew.''

Morgan believed him. It had gone far enough. Sully was starting to say something else. Morgan didn't want to hear it. He smashed Sully on the head with the heavy Colt and pushed him over the wall into the river. He heard the splash as the body hit the water.

He walked back up to Main Street and no one saw him, as far as he could tell. The rain was coming down harder than ever and even his underpants were wet. His boots squelched and he thought of hot coffee and a warm bed. He felt good about the killing of the two men. It needed to be done and he'd done it. He hadn't trusted Laura Yoder, but it wouldn't have made any difference if he had. If he'd warned her to be careful, not to be so daring, she wouldn't have listened. These emancipated women never took advice from anybody. They knew what they wanted and they went after it. Laura Yoder wanted to make a big name for herself with the Halliday story and it got her killed.

It was past two o'clock, little chance that Neal would still be in his office. But it was worth taking a look. He walked down there without meeting anyone. The newspaper building was dark except for a few dim lights. They printed the paper in the evening and delivered it the next morning. Everyone had gone home by now. It was too late to get at Neal, but there was nothing else he could have done. Newbold was just an odd job man and could have drifted out of town at any time. Same for Sully. They had to be killed while they were available.

Neal would have to wait. No drifter but a respected member of the community, a close friend of the mighty Drick Halliday, he would stay put. Tomorrow night, Morgan thought, I'll do it tomorrow night.

No use trying to get a boarding house room at this hour. They didn't take kindly to strangers knocking on their door in the middle of the night. There might be a few places that would take him in, but he didn't know where they were. He could get a room in some hotel, but somehow he didn't feel like it. The good feeling he had after killing Oscar and Sully had been replaced by a kind of edginess. He guessed it was the strain of waiting all evening to get it done.

He was hungry for food, hungry for a woman. He didn't think of the woman part until he was eating ham and eggs in a little dump that stayed open all night and catered mostly to sailors who staggered in from the saloons and whorehouses. Morgan had been there before and ate ham and eggs, which were safe, instead of a steak, which might not be.

Not all the customers were sailors. A patrolman in one of the new blue uniforms had an enormous free meal in front of him on the counter. On his plate were steak and eggs, home fried potatoes, toast, blood pudding, pancakes. This bluecoat was not going to go hungry. He gave Morgan a quick look, but was more interested in packing away the grub.

Two ranch hands, bleary eyed and still half-drunk, were moping over mugs of coffee. No one else was there.

Morgan figured he'd go to Mrs. Vega's whorehouse, get a poke, and sleep till morning. How much sleeping he'd do depended on the girl he got. The right girl could revive a man faster than a dozen cups of black coffee.

Mrs. Vega was a buxom Mexican lady who had strayed far north, but she had a fine stable of fillies. The more he thought about it, the more he liked it. A warm bed, a nice uncomplicated whore. The session with Laura Yoder had been all right and would have been better if not for the tension between them. The business with the treacherous Nez Perce woman was peculiar, to say the least.

Mealymouths who condemned whorehouses didn't know what they were talking about. Unless you wandered into the wrong place, a well run whorehouse could be a refuge, a safe haven, a place to hide from the world's woes. Best of all, there was no soul-searching in a whorehouse. Civilian women, as the whores called them, brought too much emotional baggage to bed. All too often, while you were poking them, you had to listen to stories about their brutal or adulterous husbands, or their gentlemen friends who kept dodging the married state. In a whorehouse you paid for what you got. You got no dogs in the decent places. And once you paid for your whore, you could do anything you liked with her. She'd suck you off or take it in the ass, all part of the job.

Morgan had reasoned himself into a real hard-on by the time he finished his meal. Mrs. Vega's was down by the bridge that spanned the Clearwater. Her place was a four story brick building that had been a hotel in the boom days of the '60s, and it was said that she managed to buy it only with the help of Col. Fisk, venerable president of a local bank and a cocksman of some repute despite his years and the silver headed can he used to prop himself up.

Morgan walked briskly but not because of the rain. Now that he had made up his mind, he wanted to get to it. Mrs. Vega liked to please her guests, as she called them, and she would get somebody to hang up his clothes to dry while he fucked or slept. You could buy drinks at Mrs. Vega's. The prices were high, but you didn't get bad beer or gut-burner whiskey.

The houseman opened the door and regarded him with some disfavor. He knew he must look like a drowned rat. Mrs. Vega's was on the elegant side and some of her guests, usually the elderly, arrived there in glossy conveyances.

The houseman looked capable, but wasn't the usual

thug. He eyed Morgan carefully, not sure he wanted to let him in.

"Yes, sir, what can we do for you?"

"I got caught in the rain."

"I can see that, sir."

Morgan said, "Mrs Vega may not remember me, but I've been here before. A man named George had your job then. That was two years back."

"George died," the houseman said. "Won't you come in, sir."

It was nice to get out of the rain and into a warm house with its comforting smell of women. The houseman took Morgan's lined canvas coat and said he would get somebody to hang it up to dry in the laundry room.

"Later we'll dry the rest of your clothes, sir, as soon as you're comfortable. Just put them on a chair outside the door. They'll be quite safe."

He was a discreet, well-spoken houseman, and Morgan wondered where Mrs. Vega found him. Maybe he was a butler who had invested his life savings in Mrs. Vega's operation. He was in his fifties, but looked as if he could handle himself.

In spite of the late hour, Mrs. Vega was up and around. The houseman showed Morgan into her office. Here the rule was pay first and fuck later, if you weren't a steady john. Mrs. Vega had a pretty face and a lot of lard on her short body. She wore a black dress with silver threads in it.

"Welcome," she said. "I think I know you, but you haven't been in lately. You have been neglecting us, you naughty man." She spoke good English with just a trace of a Mexican accent. "Your lady for the night was Baby, a lovely girl. Alas, she is no longer with us. She married a very wealthy man."

Morgan wanted to get out of his wet clothes. He paid for a woman he hadn't seen yet, and he gave Mrs. Vega his gun. She hung it on a pegged rack with other guns.

"All my young ladies are wonderful," Mrs. Vega said smugly. "Come into the parlor and see for yourself."

Chapter Eight

Not many "guests" were willing to come out on such a miserable night and the parlor was filled with good looking young whores sitting around with nothing to do. This part of whoring always caused Morgan some embarrassment. It was a little like a horse auction. In most places, the whores got a commission for every man they fucked, as well as their regular pay packet, and they all wanted to work.

He picked a pretty, dark-haired girl who looked to be no more than 17. God forgive him, he liked them even younger than that, but 17 was all right. At 17, unless they'd started at 14, most whores hadn't hardened into mechanical fuck-makers.

The other whores smiled as they'd been taught to do, but Morgan knew they were disappointed that he hadn't chosen one of them. It was one of his dreams, especially when he had a good load of beer on, that someday he'd have enough money to pay for all the women in a house, then get them all into a big room with a thick carpet on the floor, strip them naked and fuck and suck and bugger to his heart's content. The undertaker could come for him in the morning.

For now he was happy to have this pretty girl walking up the stairs with him. She had a soft voice and seemed shy. That could be a pose—some men liked their whores to be virginal—but Morgan didn't care. This was how he liked sex to be. You paid for a woman, treated her with respect, and went away satisfied. It was a good arrangement. The man got fucked and the girl made money. There was nothing sordid about it. A whore in a good house had a much better life than a foot-weary waitress or a farm girl slopping hogs. Looking at the shapely rump of the young girl leading him up to her room, he thanked God for whores, what would life be without them.

It was a nice room, small but clean, with curtains on the window, a rug on the floor. He took off the girl's dress and she helped him to get out of his wet clothes. She hung his clothes over the back of the only chair in the room and put the chair out in the hall. His body was damp and she rubbed it with a towel from the washstand. Lord that felt good, especially when she got down around his cock and balls.

Morgan knew he didn't smell so good after the ride to and from the mission.

"I'm going to give you a bed bath," she said, wrinkling her nose, but smiling to take the harm out of it.

She filled a washbasin with water from an enamel pitcher, lathered a wash cloth with soap, and washed him all over. The soap smelled good and so did she. She made him turn over so she could wash his back, ass, and legs. Then she dried him so hard, rubbed so vigorously, his skin tingled. This was the life, he thought. It couldn't get much better than this. He thought of Oscar and Sully, their bodies being carried along by the Snake's swift currents.

To each his own: them for the river, me for this.

The girl got onto the bed beside him and he asked her what they called her. He liked to have some name for the women he fucked. It didn't have to be a real name, anything would do.

"Suzie," she said. "Short for Susanna. I don't like it. Sounds silly, like that old darky song. What do they call you? Don't tell me if you don't want to."

"Most people call me Morgan, my last name."

"Pleased to meet you, Morgan," she said, and they both laughed.

God damn! He'd made a good choice with this little gal. She was little all right, no more than five-two, but what there was of her was put together just right. She had a shapely body and her skin had the freshness of youth. He felt like licking her creamy breasts, and so he did. He licked his way down to her cunt and got his tongue into her. He couldn't tell if the way she moaned and squirmed was the real thing. Not many whores, even the young ones, were excited by sex, at least not while they were doing it professionally. Off duty, so to speak, with a man they loved, they could be as passionate as any woman.

Morgan tasted petroleum jelly as he tongued her clit, and he raised up from his sucking and slid his rigid cock into her. It was so satisfying, the smooth way it went in. Her cunt hadn't been fucked enough to become slack, something that happened to older whores. So it was still tight and had an elastic feel to it. A tight cunt and a big cock gave a man a lot of pleasure. Lord, but wasn't this better than standing out in the cold rain. He thought how pleasant it would be to stay here and fuck this lovely girl for a week. Send down for sandwiches when you got hungry, for beer when you raised a thirst. You could get most anything at Mrs. Vega's, provided you could pay for it.

But that was not to be, at least not this trip. Duty called and God damn Halliday and his Indian war. After he took care of Neal, he would head on down to Grangeville to take a look at Halliday's biggest trading post. The guns at the mission had come from one of Halliday's trading posts, so it was possible that guns were going to other tribes, not just the Nez Perce. Halliday was taking a big risk giving guns to the Indians, even a few guns, and if the people in the territory ever found out about it, he'd be lucky if he wasn't lynched.

Lynching Halliday was a fine idea, but how was proof to be found? Who would testify against him? The kid's idea, dragging the Indian woman down to Boise, wouldn't work. Any statement she made to Gen. Howard would be torn to shreds. Morgan himself was ready to make a statement, ready to lie his head off about the guns, but he was known to be a friend of the general. They would dig that up if they didn't know it already and his testimony would be regarded with suspicion if not downright disbelief.

Suzie cut in on his thoughts. "Don't I please you, Morgan?"

"Course you do."

"Then prove it, big man. Your mind is a million miles away."

"I was thinking how nice it is here with you, the cold rain coming down outside."

"That's the nicest thing anybody ever said to me."

Morgan put Halliday out of his mind and concentrated on fucking this sweet young whore. That was what he had come here for and he put all his energy into it. If she did it according to the whore's book of tricks, she did it extremely well. He fucked her with her legs wide open, then she wriggled around until her short legs were hanging over his shoulders. He had to raise her up before he could fuck her that way.

He fucked her every way he could think of, driving it into her from behind. Her ass was round and firm yet soft. He fucked her in the mouth. He didn't just lie there and let her suck his cock. She sucked it sure enough, but he pumped his cock in and out of her mouth while she was doing it. Her puckered-up lips felt just like a small cunt. Not knowing what to do next, he went back to fucking her in the cunt, the first love of every man who loves women.

The tension was building up in him. He didn't want to stop, but it was getting to the point where he could no longer control himself. His balls tightened up for the come that could not be held back any longer. Driving into her all the way, he shot his load of hot, sticky juice. He gave her short thrusts as he came and he kept on doing that until he couldn't do anything more but lie there on top of her, happily exhausted.

Still on top of her, thinking back, he couldn't recall when he'd had a more satisfying come. Of course, part of it was the complete freedom he had enjoyed with her. He had done things to her that he would have hesitated to try with someone like Laura Yoder. Poor Laura, a honey, as the kid called her. She might not have minded being fucked in the mouth if she had come to know him better.

He yawned and Suzie smiled at him. "You're still tensed up, Morgan. I could feel it in your shoulder muscles. What have you been doing with yourself?"

"Working very hard. It gets to you."

"What you need is a good massage. Turn over."

Morgan turned over and put his face in the pillow. Her hands were small but strong and she kneaded his shoulder muscles and thumped his back with her fists until he felt as weak as a newborn kitten. He tried to fight against sleep, but it was no use. He drifted off into comforting darkness.

He had no idea what time it was when he woke up. It wasn't morning yet. There was no light at the window. Suzie was in bed beside him, reading the *City & County News*.

"My Lord, how you slept, Morgan."

"I needed it." Morgan stretched. "What time is it? My watch is on the table."

"A few minutes past five. It's still raining, not as heavy as it was. Heavy enough. You paid for all night so why don't you stay? Your clothes are dry and your shirt and drawers were washed and ironed. See there on the chair. You'll get all wet again if you leave before the rain stops."

The last thing Morgan wanted was to leave this warm bed. "I'm not leaving. What makes you think I was?"

"Oh, you wanted to know what time it was."

"I slept so sound I wanted to get my bearings."

"I'm glad you're staying all night. If you left I'd have to go back down to the parlor. There's nobody out tonight and I'd have to sit there and twiddle my thumbs till eight o'clock. That's when I get off. You want to . . . ?"

"In a little while." Morgan was still drowsy from the short but deep sleep and was content to just lie there until he felt like another fuck.

"Take it easy," Suzie said. "You have hours yet. Want to look at the paper. William leaves it at my door every night after he reads it."

Morgan had no interest in the paper, but Suzie held it up anyway. He was about to say, "Not right now" when he caught Neal's name on the front page. The item was in a ruled box that set it apart from the rest of the news. He took the paper from her and smoothed out the creases. The item was titled: EDITOR NEAL TO ATTEND IDAHO PARTY CONFERENCE IN BOISE. The title was in two lines and below it was a brief report:

S.D. Neal, editor of this newspaper, left town yesterday to attend a week-long conference of the Idaho Party, the new political organization, to be held in Boise. Founded by the well known businessman, Cedric W. Halliday, the Idaho Party is dedicated, in his words, "to all the right thinking citizens of this territory." The conference, Mr. Halliday says, is in response to Gen. Oliver Howard's efforts to organize a mass meeting to protest the Idaho Party's demand that all the Indian tribes be removed from this territory, in the interests of peace and progress, and settled in a more suitable location. Gen. Howard, a veteran of the Civil War, commanded the regular army and militia troops during the Nez Perce War of 1877. Editor Neal has been the offical historian of the Idaho Party since it was organized in January of this year. In his absence, his duties will be performed by Managing Editor Finley Dobson.

The news of Neal's departure was a jolt. He was all set to kill the bastard in less than 24 hours and now he had to wait. He could follow him to Boise and kill them there, but that would be a dumb move. The idea had been to kill Neal from ambush, shoot him with a rifle through his office window or when he left the building. Kill him and hope to get away with it. He wanted to see a headline in the *News* that read: EDITOR NEAL KILLED BY UN-KNOWN ASSASSIN. Something like that. He didn't want to have the law after him for the rest of his life. Spade Bit was waiting for him and he wanted to go back there when this Goddamned business was over.

Even if he abandoned everything and went to Boise to kill Neal, getting him in his sights wouldn't be so easy. Not with all those people around. He might even get caught or killed and that would put Gen. Howard in the cesspool. Much as he hated to do it, he would have to wait for another day.

Suzie was playing with his cock and he turned his attention back to her. In a way he was glad not to have to kill Neal so soon. Too much sneaky killing could get on a man's nerves. It would be a relief to ride down to Grangeville, get off by himself, not have to talk to anybody, at least for a while. Every once in a while he liked to get away from people, and even back at Spade Bit there were times when he felt hemmed in. When that happened, he had to get on his horse and dodge off for a while.

Suzie stroked his cock until it came up like a flagpole. She opened her legs and he got it all the way in with one vigorous thrust. This would have to be his last paid poke for some time and he was determined to make the most of it. He'd done all his fancy fucking earlier. This would be a straight fuck. Sometimes that was as enjoyable as the fancy stuff. Man on top of woman, cock in cunt, there was a lot to be said for it.

Her hands roamed all over him and she whispered words of encouragement. He didn't need encouragement, but he liked to hear what she said. What he liked most about her was that she didn't put on the usual jaded whore's performance, saying, "Oh my God, I've never seen a man with such a big one. I'm afraid of it, it's so big. I swear it must hang down to your knees." Bullshit like that. It could be funny if you didn't hear it too often, but Morgan had heard it too often. Most men liked to be told how big they were, Morgan did not. He knew how big he was and took no particular pride in it. But he had to admit, it was better than being small.

One last thrust made him come deep inside her. Suzie pretended to come, but didn't overdo it. She gasped and quivered and then lay under him with her eyes closed. Morgan knew he'd have to leave pretty soon. There was light at the window, so it had to be about six o'clock or shortly after. As soon as he had breakfast, he would get his horse and head southeast toward Grangeville. It was a good ride, but there was no reason to hurry. There was no way the kid could beat him there. He might even have to kill a day or two before the kid arrived with news from Boise.

Morgan got dressed, but Suzie stayed in bed. "Mrs. Vega must be asleep by now, so maybe I can stay here till eight o'clock. If she doesn't bother me by eight, I can sleep all day."

"Good luck to you." Morgan put a ten dollar bill on the dresser before he left. He couldn't afford such a big tip, but what the hell!

The whores in the parlor were dozing when he got downstairs. Outside, the rain had stopped, but the sky was dark and low as if it would rain again before long. Main Street was deserted except for a man driving a wagon and a municipal worker putting out the gaslamps. The town looked wet and dreary, as if the sun never shined. In the old days, Morgan used to like Lewiston well enough. Now he didn't.

Laura Yoder would always be a bad memory.

He ate a quick breakfast in the all-night restaurant, the only place open at that hour. Ham and eggs, three cups of black coffee. A solitary sailor was asleep, his head on the counter. The proprietor was getting nasty about it. Morgan threw money on the counter and left.

He had to cross the bridge again, to pick up the road that went southeast to Grangeville. He had been over this road in years past. It was getting on near to seven o'clock and wagons were coming in from the farm country. The sky was clearing and it looked as if it might not rain after all.

He knew the first sizable town would be Craigmont. Halliday had a trading post there and it was worth a look, but like the kid said, he couldn't just walk in and start asking questions. What he'd do was go in and buy something, get the feel of the place. It wasn't much of a plan, but it was all he could think of.

Craigmont was about 50 miles from Lewiston and there

was no way he could make it in one day. In the late afternoon he ate a fresh ham sandwich and drank a bottle of beer in a tiny place called Reubens. Six houses, a general store, the saloon he ate in, a Baptist meeting hall. The fresh ham wasn't so fresh, but the beer was all right. He moved on.

It started to get dark. Rain was threatening again and he had to find a place to sleep. In the end, he settled for the underside of a wooden bridge that spanned a sluggish creek. Under the bridge wasn't so bad. There was a fair-sized space, weedy but fairly dry, between the creek and the foundations of the bridge. The horses had room enough if they didn't crash around too much. He grained and watered the horses and they settled down pretty good. It started to rain, again.

He had bacon and beans, but nothing to start a fire with. He was hungry after the long ride from Lewiston. Eating cold beans from the can was as good as he could do. After he finished the beans, he chewed on raw bacon. What he missed most was good hot black coffee. Bread might be the staff of life, according to the wise men, but coffee was coffee.

He checked on the horses before he rolled himself in his blankets. At least it was dry under the bridge. With the rain pelting down, he could have been in a worse place. But he sure missed that coffee.

He slept all night and the rain had stopped by the time he rolled his blankets. For breakfast he chewed biscuits and drank water. The light was still thick when he started out again.

He figured to get to Craigmont about noon. The sky cleared and the sun showed itself before he was halfway there. They would have coffee in Craigmont. The sun got hot and started to dry out the country. Maybe it was done raining for a while. Rain might be good for the crops, but he hated it.

In Craigmont he got his coffee in a five-stool place run by an old man with a wooden leg. A Civil War veteran and proud of it, he had decorated his beanery with bits and pieces from the war. A cavalry saber, an old Springfield cavalry carbine, a rusty percussion revolver, a faded regimental flag. He was good and drunk and Morgan figured his true story might be that he had lost his leg falling under the wheels of a streetcar.

Drunk or not, he made good coffee, thick and black and strong. He recommended the beef stew and Morgan decided to take a chance on it. It was light on the beef, heavy on the potatoes, onions and carrots, but it was hot and tasted good. Morgan passed on the apple pie, the blueberry pie, the rice pudding. But he drank a fourth cup of coffee before he left.

Halliday's trading post was across the street from the old man's place. Morgan watched it all the time he was eating. There wasn't much to see. It looked no different from hundreds of trading posts all over the Northwest.

This one was doing a fair business, though the great days of trading skins were over. Years back the dumbhead trappers had all but wiped out the beaver. Just as the bird-brain hunters had slaughtered the buffalo on the plains. These days, trading posts did more business in blankets, firearms and ammunition, than they did in skins.

Morgan went in and bought a box of cartridges for the rifle so he could take a look at the place. The wall behind the counter facing the door had racks for rifles and shot-guns, pistols hanging on pegs by their trigger guards. They had a single Winchester lever-action shotgun, a new weapon, on display. Under it was a hand-lettered card saying it could be ordered from the factory, prompt delivery guaranteed. Morgan had heard bad reports on this weapon. The lever-action didn't grip the cartridges right. All in all, a lever-action shotgun didn't seem like such a good idea.

104

He skipped the trading posts in the next two towns he rode through, and it was nearly dark when he got to Grangeville, a place of some size. Smaller, narrower streets branched off the main one. It had two banks, three churches, many stores. The biggest was a department store owned by Jacob Stein & Sons. C.W. Halliday's trading post was at the end of town, standing by itself with plenty of space on both sides of it. Across the street from it was an old hotel in need of paint. The hotel and the trading post looked as if they'd been there since the town was a village.

Most of the stores in town were closed. The trading post was still open, a few horses hitched in front of it, a farm woman sitting in a wagon, holding the reins. Morgan didn't go in. Time enough to do that by daylight. First a room in the hotel and, with God's grace, maybe something to eat.

He had to slam the desk bell hard before the clerk appeared from somewhere out in back. He was a small, middleaged man in need of a shave, in his shirtsleeves. The celluloid collar to the shirt unfastened and the tie hanging down. The hotel needed paint, the clerk needed a bath. Morgan didn't care.

Sure they had a room for him, the clerk said. They had any number of rooms, big and small. Morgan said he wanted a room facing the street so he'd have plenty of light. The clerk took no notice of that, at least Morgan hoped he didn't. There were three vacant rooms facing the street, the clerk said. He could take his pick. The clerk was eager to please. Maybe he wasn't a clerk, maybe he owned the place. All the rooms were the same, all very nice.

Finally, Morgan paid for a room and got a key. The room was on the second floor, small and dusty, and a tear in the oiled-paper window shade had been repaired with gummy tape. There was the usual scarred dresser, a chair but no table. The head and foot of the bed were plated brass, and the bed itself sagged in the middle. Morgan had been in a hundred hotel rooms just like it.

It was dark in the room, the only light coming from the trading post across the street. A kerosene lamp stood on the dresser, but he let it be for now. The window shade was pulled down most of the way. The spring was broken and he had to stand on the chair to roll it up. He pulled the chair back from the window and sat on it. From where he was he had a clear view of the trading post. The recent rain had washed the outside of the window clean. The glass on the inside was smudged and dusty and he gave it a few licks with the end of the bedsheet. That would do well enough. He couldn't just sit there, looking out of a too-clean window. What he expected to see he didn't know. But this was the biggest of Halliday's trading posts, and it would have the most guns. Something could be happening there.

No way to know if Halliday took an active interest in the string of trading posts started by his father. Halliday had bigger money-makers, a lot bigger, so a manager could be looking after this part of the overall business. Morgan would sit and watch, all he could do for now. Anyway, he had to wait for the kid.

He pulled the shade down all the way before he lit the lamp. Then he went downstairs and asked the clerk, who had to be summoned with more bell banging, where he could stable his horses for the night. The clerk said there was a stable out back where his guests put their animals. There was no extra charge for the hay or the water from the pump.

"What about something to eat?" Morgan said. "Town is closed up for the night."

The clerk considered the problem. "Well, I can fix you something, or you can do it yourself. Kitchen's out back. We used to do pretty considerable in the food trade before the slump in the hotel business.''

Morgan could see why there might be a slump in *his* business. He was in a bad location, but that wasn't all of it. Outside, the peeling paint made the place look like it was ready to fall down. Inside, the lobby, the desk top, the rooms, everything, had a good coat of dust. Morgan kind of liked the little bastard. He looked defeated by life and the hotel business.

Morgan said he'd cook for himself after he saw to the horses.

"Larder's sort of bare," the clerk said. "But you'll find some canned goods, beans, tomatoes, peaches, and the like.''

"No porterhouse steak?"

"You must be joking. If I had any, I'd eat it myself.''

Morgan wanted to look at the stables. He wouldn't put the horses there if they were dirty. But they were all right and he figured some poor odd job man took care of them. Surely not the clerk or proprietor, who looked as if he didn't do much of anything.

Morgan pumped water into the horse trough and forked down hay. Then he latched the stable door securely. He took his grub to the desk, his saddle and rifle up to his room. When he came down again, the little man called from the kitchen, "In here, back here.''

Morgan went to look for him.

Chapter Nine

After a fair meal of bacon, beans and dehydrated potatoes cooked on a dusty cast iron stove, with canned peaches for dessert, he went back up to his room. He took a pot of coffee with him. Coffee never kept him awake if he wanted to sleep.

He blew out the lamp, rolled up the window shade, and sat on the chair watching the trading post. The farm wagon was gone, so were two of the three horses. By the time he finished a cup of coffee, a man came out of the trading post, got on the remaining horse, and rode away. The trading post closed up right after that.

A slightly built woman stood in the lighted doorway for a moment while a man came out to put up the shutters. Morgan couldn't tell how old she was but she looked young.

He might as well turn in for the night but he was up at six the next morning. The trading post wasn't open yet. What was left of the coffee was cold, but it was drinkable.

Morgan's Squaw

The trading post opened at seven. The same man took down the shutters and opened the double door wide. The woman he'd seen the night before came out and swept the double door wide. She was very young, about 18 or 19, and she looked angry. He picked up the old binoculars so he could see her better.

Well yes, she was angry all right, angry and sullen, with a blank stare of discontent. Her hair was straw colored and her eyes were light blue. She was fairly tall and had a figure the loose grey dress didn't do much to hide. Her face was sullen but beautiful, sort of round with a pointed chin, which gave her an unusual look. Morgan wondered who she might be. The daughter of the man he'd seen? His wife? The man looked to be in his fifties, far too old for a woman like that. Just the same it was possible. If the man was making good money, the girl might not care about his age. A farm girl or a poor town girl might think him a good catch. But she didn't look like a poor town or farm girl. Morgan was sure of that, the longer he watched her through the binoculars.

There was a sort of grace about her, a touch of elegance that showed through even while she was sweeping the porch. Some poor women had natural grace, not many though. It was clear to Morgan that she didn't like this sweeping chore. But maybe it was just the old story of a young woman marrying a much older man and living to regret it.

The man, whoever he was, came out of the trading post, shaking his finger, dressing her down. She just stared at him. He grabbed the broom away from her and gave the porch a couple of strokes, showing her how to sweep. Instead of taking the broom back from him, she flounced into the store. That was the right word for what she did: she flounced. The man followed her and that was the last Morgan saw for a while.

He was cooking a quick breakfast when the clerk came

into the kitchen. He looked as if he'd slept in his clothes. Maybe he drank. Maybe he was too world weary to get undressed. He still hadn't shaved and if he went a few more days without the razor he'd have the beginnings of a nice ratty beard.

"Coffee smells good," he said.

"Help yourself," Morgan said, turning over bacon in the pan.

The clerk poured coffee and sat at an old pine table marked up by long use. "Good coffee. My name is Alfred Jenkins. I'm afraid I didn't get yours. You didn't sign the register."

"It's Morgan."

He knew what was coming and headed it off. "I'm in the horse business up north. Heading down to Boise, but maybe I'll stop here a few days. How is the horse business in these parts?"

Jenkins sipped his coffee. "To be honest with you, I haven't a clue."

"Nothing lost by looking around." Morgan forked the bacon and beans onto a plate and took it to the table. "There's more bacon. You're welcome to it."

"Coffee is fine for now." Jenkins paused. "Guess you're surprised to see a man like me running a rundown hotel in a town like this."

Morgan didn't know what to say. There was nothing special about this seedy man. "Well, you don't exactly look like a hotelkeeper."

Jenkins was pleased. "I'm glad you said that. I was in San Francisco reading law in a lawyer's office when my father died and I came back to sell the place. Nobody wanted to buy and so I stayed on, thinking maybe I'd run it for a while until I found a buyer. And I stayed on and on. Some money was left from my father's estate so life was easy enough. The money's long gone and here I am twenty years later. I can't seem to get started again."

And you never will, Morgan thought. "Saw a mighty pretty girl sweep the porch over yonder. The trading post. Early this morning."

"I've seen her." Jenkins wasn't too interested.

"Any idea who she is?"

"I haven't a clue. They mind their business and I mind mine. Maybe I will have some of that bacon. Usually I'm not much for cooking. Opening cans is so much easier."

Morgan left Jenkins to his bacon frying and went back to his room. It was early yet and he'd take a walk around town when it got busier.

Might as well keep an eye on the trading post until then. No sign of the sullen beauty. A big freight wagon loaded with wooden crates covered with a tarpaulin came down the street and drove around behind the trading post.

A young man, more a boy, came out of the trading post and hung a hand-lettered sign on a nail beside the door. Morgan put the binoculars on the sign. Blankets were on sale at reduced prices all week. The middle-aged man came out to look at the sign. He got down from the porch and backed into the middle of the street so he could see it from there. Something about him was vaguely familiar. He was about five-ten, stockily built, had a thick black beard clipped short, and wore a cloth cap with a button on top.

Morgan couldn't place him. The beard made him look a little like Ulysses S. Grant. But that wasn't it. A lot of stocky men with clipped beards looked like Grant. But this man did resemble somebody Morgan had seen somewhere. He gave up on it.

The room was stuffy and he opened the window about six-inches from the bottom. This sitting and watching was a pain in the ass in more ways than one. The chair was hard and straight-backed. He took the pillow from the bed and made a cushion of it. A lot better.

Once, the girl came to the door and stood there for a

few moments, shading her eyes against the sun. Then she went back inside. Had she spotted him? Morgan didn't think so. The chair was pulled back from the window. He pulled it back a little more, sat and watched.

It got to be ten o'clock and he went out for his stroll down the main street. Grangeville was a big enough town and nobody stared at him. A man with a deputy's badge did give him a look, no more than that. He went down one side of the street and came back on the other. He bought a dozen bottles of beer and carried them back to the hotel.

More waiting. The only bright thing in this dreary town was the girl. He looked forward to seeing her, wanted her to stay where he could continue to look at her. Pure foolishness. Just the same, he meant to go over there so he could see her up close, listen to how she spoke. That is, if she spoke at all. For all he knew, she might talk like an illiterate farm girl. Not that he had anything against farm girls who couldn't read or write. Some of his best fucks had been with women like that. He had no preferences in women and he'd just as soon fuck a waitress as a bishop's wife. Fucking was the great leveler, and once a woman had her clothes off and her legs spread, her place in society was of no importance.

Thinking about the girl across the street gave him a medium hard-on. An angry woman often made for a great fuck. They brought their anger to bed and quite often they got rid of it by the time they put their clothes back on. A good fuck was good for them and the man who gave it to them was doing good in the best way there was. Morgan was more than willing to do good to the angry gal over yonder. What he didn't want to get was a load of buckshot, even birdshot, for his efforts.

He was restless and now was as good a time as any to wander over there. There was only one customer in the store, a man buying a pair of waterproof boots with canvas uppers. A gawky galoot in his early twenties, he was trying to tell the girl, who was wrapping the boots, about a dance that was to be held on the following Saturday night.

"You wouldn't want to come, would you?" the hayseed said.

"No, I certainly would not," the girl said. She slammed his package down on the counter to add weight to her point.

Morgan knew a finishing school accent when he heard one. He'd fucked a few women and girls with la-di-da accents like that. Usually they acted as if they were conferring a great favor by spreading their legs. It was as if they were saying, "You may fuck me, my good man, but don't get too familiar."

Morgan couldn't help staring at her and she didn't like it. Instead of saying, "What can I do for you?, something like that, she said irritably, "What do you want?"

Morgan thought she was a very rude girl and should have her bottom spanked. And, by gum, he was just the man to do it.

The bearded man, who must have been listening in, came through a doorway with an angry look on his face. "Haven't I told you a hundred times that is no way to greet a customer."

Morgan felt he had to stick up for this bad girl. "It doesn't matter, sir."

"Well, sir, it matters to me. This is a business establishment and customers must be treated with respect." The bearded man turned to the girl. "I won't have it, Melanie."

"I'm sorry, Uncle Bob," she said, not sorry at all. She gave Morgan an insolent smile. "What can I do to help you, sir?"

Uncle Bob hadn't cooled down yet. "That's better, but say it like you mean it. We are here to serve our customers, not the other way around. Good day to you, sir.''

Uncle Bob went back to what he'd been doing and Morgan was left with Bad Girl Melanie.

''What do you want?'' she said, but she gave Morgan a reluctant smile. Then she added, ''Uncle Bob is an old auntie with a beard.'' She put on a growly voice. ''What can I do to help you, sir?''

She was such a bad girl, Morgan felt like saying, ''How about sucking my cock?'' But of course he didn't. What he said was, ''I'd like two pairs of underpants, size 36 in the waist.''

Melanie gave him a quick once-over. ''You could get into a 34 if you'd lay off the potatoes.''

Such a lovely voice, so musical, so elegant. Women's voices had a way of getting to Morgan and he felt his cock stiffen. ''Winter pounds,'' he said. ''By mid-summer I'll be down to a 34, maybe a 32.''

''How very interesting,'' she said in that drawly voice.

Morgan got his underpants, but didn't want to leave. ''You're not from around here, are you?''

''However did you guess?''

''Doesn't take much guessing to see that.''

''And where are you from? I've never seen you before.''

''I'm from up north.''

''Where up north. Canada? The North Pole?''

''I have a horse ranch north of the Clearwater River. Where are you from?''

Melanie sighed. ''If you must know, I'm from Boise. But I've been to New York, London, Paris, Rome. Have you?''

Before Morgan could answer Uncle Bob bustled in, saying, ''Go get your lunch and don't take too long about it. I have things to do.''

Morgan took his underpants and got out of there before Uncle Bob could start in on him. Back in his room, he threw the underpants in a dresser drawer, uncapped a bottle of beer, and sat down to drink it.

So the old fucker was her uncle. It was hard to put them together. The go-getter businessman and the drawling, insolent girl who had been all over the world, if you could believe her. Morgan felt sure she was telling the truth about her travels. But what the hell was she doing clerking in a trading post in a dead-end town like Grangeville? Uncle Bob didn't look like the kind of man to send a niece to finishing school, much less on a tour of Europe. Uncle Bob looked tighter than a tick with money, the kind of man who would put a girl to work at ten or twelve. Morgan told himself all this was none of his business, had nothing to do with Halliday's Indian war.

But he continued to think about her. The best explanation he could come up with was that her folks, wealthy in her earlier years, had died, leaving her nothing. Uncle Bob had taken her in, but was making her work for her bed and board. Trying to make her work was more like it, without much success. It was plain enough that she had a real hate for Uncle Bob and his ways. No more trips to Europe, no more fancy clothes, and instead of being courted by eligible and rich young men, she was pursued by country clowns, like the fellow who wanted to take her to the dance.

Morgan knew he was spinning cobwebs. Next week, *East Lynne*, the weepy old play still packing them in all over the country. But this gal didn't belong in the cast of *East Lynne*: there was nothing virtuous about her. He wondered if she'd ever been fucked and decided she had. A willful gal like that would want to try everything. Lucky were the men or boys who had spread her legs. They must have thought they were fucking a wildcat.

The day dragged on and it was dark when the trading post closed for the night. There was nothing to see, nothing to do after Morgan cooked his supper. Three other men had rooms in the hotel, one of them a permanent guest, according to Jenkins. Morgan had run into this man on the stairs. He looked like an elderly cardsharp who had lost his nerve. Morgan turned him down when he proposed a game of cards. He wanted no truck with any of them.

That night, lying on the bed, a bottle of beer close at hand, he read the local newspaper, the *Grangeville Clarion*. For a paper with such a name, it was as dull as dishwater. But there was news of Gen. Howard and his call for a mass protest meeting, which was scheduled for Sunday, June 20th. That was ten days away. Morgan wanted to be there for the meeting and if the kid didn't show up soon he was going to head for Boise.

Ten-to-one, there would be trouble at the meeting— Halliday could hardly let it go unchallenged—and Morgan wanted to be there to lend a hand. He wasn't going to allow the general to be heckled and abused by a bunch of thugs. Shandy Gibbons would be there with his fearsome 10-gauge Greener shotgun, and that was a comfort. God help the man who threw a rock at the general. Gibbons wouldn't hesitate to blow his head off. Gibbons was a mean man, but he was completely loyal to Gen. Howard, the only man he had respect for.

Morgan hoped it wouldn't come to shooting, but it wasn't too unlikely that Halliday would try to provoke an incident. Halliday was the kind of man who would gladly allow one of his thugs to be killed if his death turned people against the general and his cause. Morgan wondered what Halliday was really like. By all accounts, he was one of the most successful businessmen in the territory. Everything he ventured into paid off big. Morgan had seen him once at a political rally in Boise. That was when he was still a Republican. A big, handsome, swarthy man with black hair and a booming voice. They said he was born in North Carolina and brought to Idaho as a child. He'd be about forty-five now.

Morgan couldn't imagine what he'd do if he had Halliday's money, or even part of it. Sure as hell he wouldn't try to set himself up as the Great White Father of Idaho, which seemed to be Halliday's intent. Men who thought they knew what was good for everyone else had to be mad to some degree. Halliday's Idaho Party attracted most of the crackpots and Indian haters in the territory. A few of the real loonies didn't want the Indians removed, they wanted to make them slaves, to work in chains in the mines and lumber camps. Others, the religious nuts, thought the Indian "problem" could be solved if the redskins were forcibly converted to Christianity. The Spanish had done it in Mexico, so why couldn't it be done here. A Christian Indian was a docile Indian.

Halliday wanted none of that. He wanted the Indians gone and it didn't matter to him if they were Christians or heathens. "I will listen to no arguments, consider no compromises. We must cleanse this territory of these savages."

Morgan had heard all this from his top hand, Sid Sefton, that great reader of newspapers. At the time he couldn't work up too much interest in Halliday's blather. Now he was glad he knew something about the son-of-a-bitch.

Young Ticknor rode in the next morning. Jenkin's hotel was the first place he looked for Morgan. For all his funny ways, Morgan was glad to see him.

The kid explained why he had looked in Jenkins's hotel before the better places in town. "I knew you were tight with a buck, Mr. Morgan, and this elegant bedbug looked to be about your speed."

"Is that so?" Morgan had to smile. "What news from Boise, smart-aleck?"

The kid sat on the edge of Morgan's bed. "I have a lot to tell you. The general got in the day after I did. I have to say he looked terrible tired. A man his age, that long journey. He listened carefully to all I told him, nodding like he does, saying nothing till I got through. Then he asked me a lot of questions, all pretty sharp. I answered best I could.''

"Good for you."

"I had to explain about the lady reporter. I said you hadn't gone after her. She'd come after you, wouldn't let you alone, even followed you up to the room to ask questions.''

"What did he say to that?''

"He said she was a brave but foolish woman.''

Morgan didn't tell the kid that Laura Yoder was dead. He said nothing about killing Oscar and Sully. It was done and he was no part of it.

"What about this mass meeting?''

"You know about that?''

"It was in the papers. Scheduled for the 20th, they say.''

"Right you are," the kid said. "The general has been beating the bushes, trying to get people to attend.''

"Has he been having any luck?" Morgan asked.

"Not as much as he'd like, but he's been doing pretty good. He is Gen. Howard, after all, and a good many people will attend the meeting. I have to tell you he's been making some strong attacks on Halliday. Accusing him straight out of being the villain behind these so-called Indian attacks. He says Halliday wants to drive the Indians out for, what were his words, for personal gain. Drive them out so him and his friends can buy their land cheap. Strong talk, Mr. Morgan.''

"Strong enough," Morgan agreed.

"I'd say the general would be in some danger if he didn't have that Gibbons fella dogging around after him. A dangerous fella, that fella. Walks the streets of Boise with that 10-gauge in the crook of his arm. Suspicious of everybody, gave me the fish eye when I showed up. Like maybe I was a sneak come to do the general. Tried to take my pistol before he let me into the general's rooms at the Rathdrum. Said I couldn't come in if I didn't give up the gun.''

"Did you give it to him?"

"Hell, no. I don't give my gun to nobody. The general heard us disputing and came out to see what was going on. He remembered me from Spade Bit and told Gibbons to quit it. Gibbons did what he was told, but he didn't like it. He's like a mother hen, that Irish fucker.''

"A mother hen with a Greener 10-gauge. Has the general been threatened? Is that what you're saying?''

"He didn't say nothing to me about that. But the way Gibbons was behaving, I think he was. Threatening a man like Gen. Howard, for Christ's sake! Even I know who he is, what he's done for his country. Lost his arm trying to save the Union. I wouldn't give my little toe to save the fucking Union. I need my little toe, more than the Union does.''

Morgan smiled. The kid was lacking in patriotism, but what the hell! What had the country ever done for him? It would be hard to wave the flag if you were dragged up like him. Morgan wasn't very patriotic himself. He'd just as soon drink beer on the porch on Sunday afternoons and read about glorious battles in the newspaper. These fiery speeches, these do-or-die battles, it didn't seem to make much difference in the end.

"Did you have a good time in Boise?

"Yup.'' The kid looked smug. "I went to a whorehouse.''

"Where did you get the money?''

"Gen. Howard loaned it to me.''

"You got money from General Howard to go to a whorehouse?''

"No such thing. I told him I needed the money to get

my horse wormed. That can cost a bit.''

Morgan shook his head. The kid was growing up fast, learning to lie like the rest of the citizens. Looking at him now, it was hard to see him falling off the bunkhouse roof, or spilling creosote on new San Antonio boots. Morgan looked at his boots. They were good and dirty by now.

Morgan said, "You're a rotten, fucking liar, but I'm glad you're back."

The kid did an aw-shucks squirm. "Thanks, Mr. Morgan."

Morgan took a pull on his third beer of the day. "Let's dispense with the *mister* part of it. Call me Morgan if you call me anything. Makes me nervous, the mister. So call me Morgan. Everybody else does. Bitsy calls me boss, but he's a Chinaman and doesn't know any better."

The kid shifted his ass on the bed. "I can't call you nothing but *Mister* Morgan."

Morgan set the empty bottle down on the floor. "Why is that?"

"Because I look up to you."

"Look at me level and you won't be disappointed. Call me Morgan. That's an order."

Morgan was feeling the beer.

"On one condition," the kid said, getting up to stretch his legs.

Morgan looked at him. "What is it?"

"For you to stop calling me 'kid.' I want you to shake on it."

While they were shaking hands, somebody knocked on the door.

Chapter Ten

Morgan thought it was Jenkins and told him to come in. Melanie came in instead. She still wore the same shapeless grey dress, but it might have been a ball gown, for the elegance she gave it. Her blue eyes took in the dingy room, Morgan, the kid.

"I thought it was just you," she said to Morgan. "Now I see there's two of you."

Morgan didn't get it. "What are you talking about? What brought you here?"

Melanie said, "I was able to sneak over here because Uncle Bob had to go and have a tooth pulled. He warned me not to budge from the store, but I did."

Morgan still didn't get it. "So I see. Would you like a bottle of beer?"

She ignored the offer. "You look like a gunman," she said to the kid. "Sticks out all over you. You'd think this one"—she meant Morgan—"would be all that was needed to spy on me."

The kid tapped the side of his head as if to say this one is cracked but a real honey, so let's jolly her along. But the girl was looking at Morgan.

"How did you peg me for a gunman?" The kid was delighted with himself.

"My father hires lots of gunmen," Melanie said. "I know the type."

Good Christ! Morgan thought. It can't be.

"Who's your father?" The kid still thought the girl was a bit off and the whole thing was some kind of joke.

The question made Melanie flare up. "You know damn well who my father is. First, this one arrives"—she gave Morgan an angry look—"then you come along a few days later. If my father wants me watched, why does it take two of you to do it. Are you here to chase me down if I make a break for it?"

Morgan wanted her to say she was Halliday's daughter. Say it without prompting. If she wasn't, he didn't want to suggest it. If she was a bit nutty, she might take a name that didn't belong to her and build on it.

"We're not here to spy on you. I'm a horse rancher from up north, like I told you at the store. I'm looking around to see what's doing in the horse trade. Ticknor here works for me."

"Call me Tick," the kid said.

The girl looked at him. "The name suits you."

Morgan said, "Believe me, we're not here to spy on you."

"Then why have you been watching me. I caught on to you the first day you did it. I was upstairs and saw you. You even have binoculars. There they are on the window sill. If that isn't spying, I don't know what it is."

"I wasn't spying. You're a nice looking girl, nice to look at."

"You want me to believe you're a Peeping Tom, not a spy. What I don't understand, why did my father have to send you two. Uncle Bob watches me closely enough.''

Time to get down to cases before Uncle Bob came back from the dentist and found her missing. "Maybe we can clear this up if you tell us who your father is.''

She looked puzzled. "You mean you really don't know? You're not working for my father?''

"Cross my heart.''

"My father is Drick Halliday and I'm Melanie Halliday. I'm his only daughter and have to be watched all the time.''

A real puzzler, Morgan thought. Could be she was a little disturbed in the head and had been placed here in care of Uncle Bob. But she didn't look or sound crazy. Willful yes, crazy no.

Morgan said, "Why do you have to be watched?''

"So I won't run off. Where could I run to without money? Uncle Bob doesn't give me a dime and keeps the store money locked in a safe. He cleans out the till several times a day, so there's never more than a few dollars in it.''

Morgan waited for her to go on, but she didn't. "What did you do to be sent here?''

She gave him a long stare with her bright blue eyes. "You really want to know?''

"If you want to tell us.'' Morgan knew pressing her might make her clam up. He hoped Uncle Bob was having a long, difficult extraction.

She sat down on the bed, a few feet away from the kid. "I don't like my father,'' she said for openers. "I've never liked him. I hate him. He was very mean to my mother, used to hit her. A few years ago he must have hit her too hard and she died a week later. She was in great pain, but my father wouldn't call the doctor. He didn't say it would be bad for his political career. He didn't have to.''

Melanie asked Morgan if she could have a sip of beer.

"Just a sip," he said. "You don't want Uncle Bob smelling it on you."

Melanie tipped the bottle back and drank. "Fuck Uncle Bob, the bootlicking, gutless shit."

She was drinking too much beer and Morgan reached for the bottle.

"About my mother," she went on. "My father did call the doctor right after she died. He said she'd taken to her bed and died suddenly. She was a frail woman who found some comfort in her illnesses. The doctor didn't examine the body, why should he. He put 'heart failure' on the death certificate, and that was that."

Morgan didn't know what to say, so he said nothing.

Melanie went on with her story. "I tried to avoid my father as much as possible after that. It was awful, the two of us alone in that big house, except for the servants. Of course, he was away a good deal of the time, which was a blessing. But when he was there, I had nothing to say to him. Now and then he tried to talk to me, but I turned my back on him. Finally he packed me off to Europe with my spinster aunt, Kate. We were to stay there for six months and see all the sights. It was his way of getting me out of the way, but I didn't care. I was glad to go. I hate Boise, but that was a minor reason. I wanted to get away from my father."

Morgan decided that what she was saying was true. She said it with such intensity, and her hatred for her father seemed real.

"That's how you got to London, the other places."

She gave him a mischievous smile that made her look very young. "That's right. And I saw them on my own, without Kate fussing over me. One afternoon—it was in London, our first stop—I took what money she had, plus her jewelry, also some checks I made out to me, forged her name, and cashed at the American Bank. She had a letter of credit there, so cashing the checks was no problem. I was seventeen, but I fixed myself up to look a few years older, at least twenty-one.''

"Then what?" Morgan wanted another beer, but knew if he uncapped a bottle she'd want to drink some of it.

"I took a boat to France, a train to Paris. Nobody took much notice of me. I could have been one of those suffragettes, the women that want the vote, drink and smoke, and chain themselves to railings. I had a wonderful time in Paris. I sold Kate's jewelry and got a lot of money for it. Oh, it was wonderful, being free and on my own. Men tried to latch onto me, of course, but I was smart enough not to be suckered. I kept most of my money in the hotel safe, taking out just enough to see me through the day. But the men did swarm around me. There was one young man I had a brief fling with. He said he was a count, but I knew he wasn't. 'Who are you really?' he used to say. 'You are such a mysterious young lady.' ''

Melanie's blue eyes sparkled as she recalled this con man. "Finally I had to move on to Rome, just to get away from him. He kept on asking me to marry him, and wouldn't take no for an answer. Rome was even more wonderful than Paris. Italian men are so romantic, so passionate. I was on the Isle of Capri with a certain young man when the European Pinkertons tracked me down and took me back to New York against my will. The New York Pinkertons bundled me onto a train and didn't let me out of their sight until I was back in Boise. You can't imagine how my father behaved, Mr.—what is your name?"

"Morgan."

"He was like a madman," Melanie said. "Cursing and swearing, threatening to have me committed to an asylum for the insane. How could I do this to him, a man in his position? How could I rob my own aunt and go off gallivanting with the scum of Europe. I guess the Pinkertons didn't leave anything out of their report. He meant it about

125

the asylum, I'm sure of that, and I was afraid because I knew he could do it. Finally, he said he was going to send me up here to work in the store with Uncle Bob. No more bullshit, he said. I was to work in the store and do everything Uncle Bob told me to do. Uncle Bob would be keeping tabs on me all the time and if I tried to run away the marshal and his deputies would find me and bring me back. And into the asylum I would go. On the other hand, my father said, if I behaved myself for two full years I could return to Boise. But I'd be on probation.''

"How long have you been here?'' Morgan asked.

"Eleven months. It's been like a nightmare, nothing to do after the store closes, nobody to talk to. Uncle Bob won't even let me go for a walk. Sundays are the worst. I've often thought of killing myself.''

"You don't want to do that.'' Morgan looked out the window and saw Uncle Bob driving a buggy around to the back of the trading post. "Uncle Bob just came back. You better get out of here.''

Melanie jumped off the bed, looking scared. "I better get in while he's looking after the horse. I'll be back if I can manage it. I want to talk to you again. Goodbye, Tick.''

The kid was goggle-eyed as she went out. Morgan watched as she ran across the street and into the store.

"Holy Jesus!'' the kid said. "Did you ever hear such a story?''

"Not lately,'' Morgan said. He'd heard stories like it, but never anything so wild. Sure as shooting, it was no *East Lynne*.

The kid was indignant. "That Halliday is surely a son-of-a-bitch. Shutting a sweet gal like that away in a doghouse town. His own daughter at that. I know I was right, what I said. Somebody ought to shoot the fucker.''

Morgan opened a beer. "Don't get started on that again. I hope she can make it back. A lot of questions I want to ask her about her father.''

"You think that clerk downstairs spotted her? He could tell the uncle.''

"She probably came up the back stairs. Anyway, Jenkins has nothing to do with Uncle Bob. I doubt if he even says hello to him. Too bad Uncle Bob came back when he did. She was going good.''

Clearly the kid was much taken with Melanie. "Wasn't she though. What a life, and her not yet twenty. A year or so older than me.''

"You've been doing some figuring.''

"Nothing wrong with that, is there? Nice to meet a girl your own age. She's a bit young for you, wouldn't you say?''

"Young Tick—''

"Just Tick, if you don't mind.''

"Tick, you leave my age out of it. The young lady may prefer a man of experience. Have you ever thought of that? Let's skip that and get serious. If she hates her father that much—and I'm certain she does—she may be willing to tell us things nobody else knows. Secrets he would like to keep buried.''

Young Ticknor looked out the window as if he hoped to see the girl. Morgan didn't think that was likely. After what she'd done, she'd be keeping her head down.

The kid said, "She might not want to do that when it comes down to the wire. It's one thing to tell tales on yourself, another to spill the beans on your own father. What she told about herself, a lot of pride in that. She may balk when it comes to her father.''

Morgan knew the kid was right. Not only might she shy away from her father's secrets, she might be afraid to say anything at all. She had told about her mother's death, but that could be something she wanted to believe. A blow from Halliday's fist need not have killed his wife. A frail woman in poor health, so the daughter said, she might have been sickening to die when Halliday hit her. What was said about the mother was said in fierce anger. Morgan doubted that she'd told the story to anyone else. After being cooped up for eleven months, with Uncle Bob sneaking around after her, with nobody to talk to, she had talked freely and no doubt felt better for it. Now, thinking of that asylum for the insane, she could be having second thoughts.

What he had to do was earn her trust. Maybe he could do that if he leveled with her. It was the only way he could think of.

"I'm going to tell her we're working for Gen. Howard. Right now she doesn't know what we are. I could see she had big doubts about that looking for new stock yarn. It sounds dodgy even to me. You don't come to farm country looking for horses. She may not know that, but maybe she does. All that aside, I think we have to tell her the truth. It's the only way we can get her to trust us."

The kid cracked his knuckles and thought about it. "I don't like it, but I guess you're right. What I'd like to know, what do you plan to do with her?"

"Take her to Boise and let her talk to Gen. Howard. If she could be persuaded to appear at the mass meeting alongside the general . . . if she'd stand up and denounce her father for all his villainies, really lay into the son of a bitch, it could turn the tide against him, turn the people against him. Of course, nothing she might say will get through to the diehards. The true believers wouldn't change their minds if she produced hard evidence that Halliday murdered his wife, was a child raper and all-round degenerate. But there are others, lots of them, who support Halliday only because so many other citizens do."

"And you think this girl could un-persuade them?" The kid looked doubtful.

"It could help to do it. Get her up there and let her talk."

"Seems kind of mean, asking her to do that. There must have been a time, prob'ly when she was a little girl, when she loved her father. At least liked him."

Morgan had been thinking about that. "Maybe it is mean, but I'll do anything to stop this Indian war."

"You're a hard man, yes sir. But now, answer me this, what do you think Halliday will do when he hears his daughter is in Boise, talking to the general. He's sure to find out."

Morgan said, "That doesn't have to be if we take her into the hotel late at night, all wrapped up in shawls and such."

The kid got off the bed, looked out the window, then sat down again. It was getting to be late afternoon and fewer customers were going in and coming out of the store. One of them was a deputy marshal, a burly man with a varnished straw hat and a sagging gunbelt.

"You think that'll work?" the kid asked. "Halliday is sure to be paying some of the hotel people for information about the general. He's paying them for any sort of information, who goes up to see the general, and so forth. One little fucker, a bellboy, tried to get chatty with me. Asking me where I was from, real friendly, the runty fucker. I wanted to kick his ass, but didn't."

Morgan smiled. "I'm glad to hear you're learning to control yourself. Getting the girl in without being spotted won't be easy, but we have to do it."

The kid made a good point. "She hasn't agreed to anything yet. You're talking as if it's all set."

"I guess I am," Morgan said, "but what else can we hope for. The information you gave the general doesn't add up to much."

The kid said, "What about that marshal she talked about. Him and his deputies will be coming after us the minute that uncle of hers finds her gone. They're taking Halliday money through the uncle. Men like that will kill us to make themselves look good. My guess is they'll round up a posse of gun-happy citizens. I'm not afraid of the fuckers, but the odds will be bad if we do it.''

Morgan was surprised to hear the kid talking such sense. Or maybe he didn't want to see the girl caught and sent to the madhouse. She said that's what would happen to her if she ran off.

''They'll have to catch up to us to do any killing. And I doubt they'll follow us all the way to Boise. It's too far. The posse will turn back first, then not so much later, the marshal and his boys. The marshal doesn't just work for Uncle Bob. He works for the town of Grangeville and the citizens will want to know why he's neglecting his duties to go chasing some girl all over the country.''

The kid was still worried about the girl. ''What'll happen to her if she does make this speech, or whatever you want to call it? Even if Halliday's badmen don't grab her, she'll be without a home. With no money, what can she do?''

Morgan was getting tired of this. ''She can go far from Boise and get a job. It's been done. Maybe Gen. Howard can find her a job in Washington. I'm thinking she'll be all right. Women like that always land on their feet. If she gets to Washington, with her good looks and education, she's sure to snag a rich husband. Maybe I'll marry her myself and take her back to Spade Bit.''

The kid didn't like to be kidded. ''You're bullshitting me.''

''That I am, Tick. I'd like you to stop mooning over this girl and think how we're going to get her out of this town and all the way to Boise. You look tired, Tick. Why don't you fix something to eat, turn in early, get a long sleep.''

The kid got off the bed and stretched his arms. ''I think

I'll do that. I pushed hard to get here from Boise.''

"You did good, Tick. See you in the morning. I'm going to turn in early myself.''

Morgan wasn't tired, wasn't sleepy. What he wanted was to get rid of the kid so he could think. It was dark now, but the trading post was still open. He wouldn't light the lamp until the trading post closed for the night. That would be in about an hour and he'd watch the place until then.

The last customer left and Uncle Bob put up the shutters, went back inside and locked or barred the door. There was no sign of the girl. The lights in the store went out and a few minutes later a light came on in one of the upstairs rooms. The window was heavily curtained and he had no way of knowing whose room it was. Not much later, the light went out.

Morgan pulled down the shade, put a match to the lamp, and stretched out on the bed. He drank a beer and put the bottle on the floor. There was a lot to think about. The kid had the room next to his and he heard him going into it, the key turning in the rusty lock. A few minutes after that he heard the kid snoring his head off. The kid had come a long way from the gawk who'd turned up on his doorstep three months before.

It was past midnight and Morgan was reading the *Grangeville Clarion* and drinking the last of his beer. The door was locked and after the doorknob turned twice somebody knocked. A light knock. Morgan knew it wasn't the kid because he could hear him snoring. He picked up his gun from the dresser before he opened the door and Melanie came in. Her dress was torn and she had smudges on her face.

At first Morgan thought Uncle Bob had beaten her up. But then she said, "I climbed down a rope from my room. Uncle Bob's in the front. I'm in the back. He couldn't have heard me or he'd be screaming bloody murder by now." She looked at the beer bottle on the floor beside the bed. "Any more beer left?"

" 'Fraid not. I'd have saved you some if I knew you were coming."

Melanie sat on the edge of the bed. "I had to talk to you. I know it's a lot to ask, but will you take me to Boise when you leave here? Not to Boise itself, to the next train stop outside it, just a few miles. And I have another favor to ask, will you lend me the train fare to somewhere. I don't know when I can pay you back, but I have to get out of here."

Morgan looked at her torn dress, the smudges on her face, the way her hands shook. "Calm yourself down. What you need is a drink. Jenkins has a bottle in the kitchen cupboard. I'll go and get it, then we'll talk."

Morgan brought the bottle and a glass up to the room and poured her a short drink. She grimaced as she drank the bad whiskey. She held out the glass and he gave her another short one. She drank it and stretched out on the bed beside him.

"I'm so damn tired," she said. "I suppose it's my nerves. Will you take me to Boise. I can hide here in your room until it's time to leave."

"Look," Morgan said. "I'll take you to Boise, but first I have to tell you something. I am a horse rancher from up north, but right now I'm working for Gen. Oliver Howard. You know who he is?"

"Yes. I read the papers and Uncle Bob is always arguing about him with men who come into the store. Uncle Bob hates him, says he should be lynched. A red nigger lover, is what Uncle Bob calls him."

"A lot of people call him that, but he's a good man, the best there is."

Melanie turned to face Morgan. "What do you mean you're working for him? As some sort of spy?"

"I'm trying to gather information for him."

"Information to be used against my father?"

"That's right. How do you feel about that? He is your father, after all."

Melanie wanted another drink before she gave him an answer. Morgan gave it to her reluctantly and watched her drink it.

"Fuck my father. He's not my father," she said fiercely. "He never was a father to me. Anything you can do to destroy the bastard will be deeply appreciated by me."

Morgan could see she was tight and maybe that was all to the good. "You can help me," he said.

"Help you how?"

"By telling me things about him nobody else knows."

Melanie got closer to Morgan than she had to. "I'll tell you anything you want to know. I'd like to see the fucker in his grave."

Chapter Eleven

Melanie hiccuped. "Did you know the son of a bitch is half Indian? Well, he is. The great champion of the white race is half redskin. Half dog eater, as he calls the Indians. His father married a North Carolina Indian woman, but she died giving birth to my rotten father. I know that because his father, my grandfather, was still alive when I was a child and he told me. My grandfather wasn't ashamed of marrying an Indian. It was common back in those days."

Melanie drank the dribble of whiskey left in her glass. Morgan waited for her to go on. When he thought about it, it wasn't hard to believe what she was telling him. Halliday was dark skinned and dark haired and he did have something of an Indian look to him.

"My grandfather took the child, my rotten father, out here to Idaho. He started with one trading post, the one here in Grangeville, and went on to build a whole chain of them. He put his money into other businesses and was a very rich man before he was fifty. My rotten father

Morgan's Squaw

lacked for nothing. The best clothes, the best horses, the best schools. One of them was a military academy back East. He grew up to be a rotten, spoiled bastard, arrogant and bigoted. Even as a child I could never understand why he hated the Indians so much. It became clear when my grandfather told me about my grandmother. I don't know why he took so long to tell me. He couldn't have liked the way my father kept going on about the Indians. My father was fairly young then, but already set in his ways. My grandfather told me not to tell my father what he'd told me, and I didn't. But I despised him for being ashamed of his own mother. By hating all Indians, he was hating her as well."

For a while Melanie's thoughts seemed to be lost in the past. Then she said, "I'm very proud of being part Indian and I hate what my father is trying to do to them."

Morgan said, "Gen. Howard is trying to stop him. So am I. You can help too, if you can bring yourself to do it. If you can't, then you can't."

Melanie pressed closer to Morgan and he was very much aware of her warm, soft body. It was odd to be getting a hard-on during such a serious conversation.

"Help you how?" she asked. "Say it."

Morgan took a deep breath and let it out. "Gen. Howard has a mass protest meeting scheduled for June 20th. It's the only way he can think of to stop your father from destroying the tribes in this territory. Would you be willing to stand up with the general and tell the people what you've told me? That your father is half Indian himself, which makes him a hypocrite. Are you willing to tell what he did to your mother? Other things you may remember."

"Yes, I am," Melanie said without hesitation. "I'll do whatever you want me to do."

For once in his life, Morgan wished he didn't have a hard-on. He tried not to think about it.

"There could be danger. I suppose you know that."

"Yes. My father is quite capable of killing me, or having me killed. He loves nothing and no one but him-

135

self. If anyone belongs in an asylum, he does.''

Morgan's hard-on just wouldn't go away and he knew he was going to fuck her in a few minutes. All the signals she was giving him made that obvious. And he liked her and wanted it bad.

"I'll try to see that nothing happens to you," he said.

Melanie was pressing up against him now. "But you can't guarantee it, can you?"

"No, I can't, but I'll do my best for you."

"You can start doing it right now," she said, and started to unbutton his pants.

His cock stood up like a rod when she took it out and stroked it. Wriggling around on the bed, they got their clothes off fast. The crotch of her drawers was sopping wet when he pulled them down over her ass. So was her cunt and if ever a woman was ready, this one was. She moaned as he spread her legs and drove into her. He knew a lot of cocks had been in this woman and the thought excited him. But all the other cocks meant nothing. He was fucking her now, pumping it in and out of her, squeezing her ass with both hands, raising it so he could give it to her at a new angle of penetration. Her moaning grew louder, but Morgan didn't think about the kid in the next room. The only thing that woke the kid was a sense of danger, and there was no danger here, just two people happily fucking.

She was no talker and he liked that. Her moaning said how much she appreciated his cock, and he liked that too. And he appreciated her cunt just as much. It was slick and hot and juicy. Sweat glistened at the edge of her straw colored hairline and all over her body. He sucked one breast, then the other, and she gasped with pleasure. She was a healthy young animal and completely unashamed. That was the best part of it, the way she showed how much she was enjoying it.

After a while, she let it be known by hand movements and whispers, that she wanted to get on top of him. Morgan liked it that way. He liked it any way, and he rolled over until she was lying on top with his cock sticking up straight into her.

"Now I'm fucking you," she whispered.

"Fuck me good then," Morgan whispered back, and that made her giggle.

And she did fuck him, in her way. She raised herself up and down on his big, long, hard cock and it was Morgan's turn to groan with pleasure. The thought came to him how odd it was to have Drick Halliday's daughter sitting on his cock. But he forgot all about it when suddenly she started to come. It started with violent contractions of her cunt, then she began to jump like a trout caught at the end of a line. She pushed down so hard on his cock, he thought she was going to hurt herself. She cried out with pain, or pleasure, or both, and he felt her hot cunt juice wetting his crotch. The bittersweet smell of come seemed to fill the room and he started to come himself. He shot his load up into her and felt some of it dribbling back down.

"Oh Lord!" she said, rolling off him. "I have to rest for a while."

They lay together face to face, temporarily exhausted by their tender struggle. It was late now and rain was pattering on the window. It was nice to be in bed with a lovely woman on such a night.

Morgan didn't want to say it, but he did. "I think we should start for Boise right now."

"What?" She was startled.

"It's late but not too late. It's raining hard and Uncle Bob is sleeping. The marshal and his boys must be doing the same. The town is closed down for the night. If we start now, we can put some miles behind us before Uncle Bob wakes up, finds you gone, and goes running to the marshal. What do you say? It's a good night to make a break."

"Oh Lord!" Melanie said. "I don't even have a coat, a raincoat, any kind of coat."

"Neither do I. Neither does Tick. We should have but

we don't. I have a rubber groundsheet in my bedroll. I can wrap that around you, give you my hat. Nothing will keep you completely dry, the way it's raining, but you won't be too bad off. Come on now, time's awasting. Yes or no?''

"All right, let's be off, sink or swim." Melanie got off the bed and started to get dressed.

Morgan did the same. "Be right back. I'm going to wake the kid.

Melanie laughed nervously. "He isn't going to like it, the way he's been snoring.''

Morgan knocked on the kid's door and found a gun pointing at him when the key turned in the lock and the door swung back. The kid let the hammer down when he saw Morgan. He was wearing longjohns, the ones with the trapdoor in back. No yawning, no blinking, he was fully awake.

"Get dressed and make it quick. Melanie is in my room and we're starting for Boise right now. Come in and say hello to her. I'll explain what's been happening. Get a move on.''

Morgan went back to his room and the kid came in a minute or two later. Melanie said, "Hello, Tick," and the kid got all bashful. He listened while Morgan explained the situation.

"All right," he said, "but will you listen to that rain.''

"All the better," Morgan said. "Not a fit night out for man nor beast. Come on, Tick, we've got to get this lady wrapped up in a groundsheet, best we can do to keep her more or less dry.''

Morgan picked up his hat and put it on Melanie's head. A stockman's hat looked funny with a grey dress, torn or otherwise. He rolled up the window shade so there was some light in the room. Then he blew out the lamp and filled two beer bottles with the kerosene in the bowl of the lamp. The bowl was nearly full and he filled the bottles right to the top. Then he tore two strips from the bedsheet and plugged the top of the bottles.

Waiting in the half dark, the kid said, "What are you doing?"

"There's a bridge over a river about ten miles south of here. River will be flooding with all this rain. We'll burn the bridge once we're across. No sane man would try to swim his horse across, the way the river must be by now. The marshal may take money from Uncle Bob, but he won't want to die for him."

Morgan turned to Melanie. "What time will Uncle Bob expect to see you in the store?"

"Seven o'clock on the dot."

"It's two o'clock now. That gives us a five hour start. We'll walk the horses out nice and quiet, then make what good time we can. You can ride behind me, later get up behind Tick. We'll spell the horses like that so they won't get tired with the extra weight."

The trading post was dark and silent, no lights showing, as they walked the horses past it. Up behind Morgan Melanie huddled in the rubber groundsheet. He could feel her shivering. He wondered what she was thinking. Not so long ago she had been living in a fine house with all the comforts. Now she was, in a way, running for her life. It was strange, the twists and turns of a person's life.

It was a good enough road, but it was dark and the rain made it worse. Out past town Morgan set his horse to moving at a fair clip, but he knew they couldn't push it too hard, not on a night like this. Anything at all could spook the horses and then they'd be in big trouble. If one of the mounts broke a leg, or one of them got thrown and took a bad fall, it would pretty much be the end of them. They could survive the loss of the pack horses, but they'd have to go without food till they hit some town. And the time wasted looking for a store to buy supplies would slow them down, not by much, but any time lost would have to be made up, if they could do it.

There was no telegraph line between Grangeville and Boise. Usually the lines ran where the railroad ran, and there was no railroad between the two towns. So there was no way Uncle Bob could tell Halliday that his daughter had run off. Morgan hoped burning the bridge would be enough to stop the marshal, his deputies, the citizen posse the marshal would be sure to round up. But he wasn't counting on it all the way. There could be a ferry at some other point on the river. He knew of no such ferry, but that didn't mean it didn't exist. Still and all, anything that slowed the marshal down would give them that much more time.

They got to the bridge Morgan remembered and the river it spanned was in full flood. The light was bad, but he was able to make out uprooted trees being carried past by the fast moving water. They crossed the bridge and Morgan told the kid and Melanie to take the horses on a bit while he went back to burn it.

"I'll catch up to you," he said.

Soaked to the skin, he ran back to look at the bridge. Wind driven rain swept the bridge, no chance of starting a fire on the topside of it. He slid, half fell down the muddy bank to get under the wooden span. It was pitch black under the bridge and he could hear but couldn't see the river rushing by.

Working blind, he unrolled the blanket. Parts of it were damp, but it wasn't soaked through. He unplugged the beer bottles and soaked the blanket with kerosene. Then he jammed the blanket up into one of the criss-cross supports that held up the bridge. He wished he could place the blanket out closer to the middle of the bridge. No way to do that.

He reached down and took a sulfur match from the lining of his boot. The matches he kept there were, like the two gold double eagles he kept in the same place, for emergencies. If the match didn't light, it would be worse than an emergency.

He struck the match on the bridge support and held his breath as it slowly caught fire. He touched it to the kerosene soaked blanket and he had to jump back as the blanket blazed up, shooting out flames in all directions.

He climbed back up the bank and waited at the end of the bridge. If the bridge didn't start to burn, there wasn't much point trying it again.

It took a while before flames began to lick through the cracks in the bridge. And then it began to burn in earnest. The flames ran out under the bridge and he could hear the crackling of the wood as it caught fire. Soon the bridge, wet though it was, was burning from end to end. He waited until the middle of the bridge collapsed before he ran to catch up with the others.

A quick swig of water was what he needed and he took it. They started off again and after another five miles Melanie got up behind the kid and wrapped her arms around his waist, as she had done with Morgan.

Morgan smiled to himself. The kid must like having her so close to him. After they were about about 20 miles from Grangeville they got down from the horses and let them rest. In spite of the rain the horses drank from the pools of water beside the road. They drank some water themselves. The thought that sudden death might not be far off always made you thirsty. It was funny to be drinking water, with the rain pelting down.

Morgan asked Melanie how she was and she said she was all right. "We have to keep going right through the night," Morgan told her. "It's the start of a getaway that counts. The more miles you can make then count more than all the others."

Still shivering with cold, Melanie tried to make a joke of it. "You've been chased a lot, have you?"

"I've been chased some," Morgan said. "I think we're going to make it. After it gets light we'll try to find a place to rest up, maybe get a few hours sleep. The horses have been going good and they need rest more than we do. Rest and grain and water."

In the morning, on about seven, they came to an abandoned farmhouse not far off the road. The roof of the house had collapsed at one end. The rest of it was still in place, sagging, but still there. A barn out back was in better shape and they stabled the horses there after they were grained and watered at a trough that had to be cleared of dead leaves before they could drink. The barn door had a bad sag to it and Morgan and the kid had to drag it before it would close.

Inside the house there were hornets' nests and not much else. The hand pump at the sink brought up rusty water at first, then it cleared and they found it drinkable. The stove was gone. The chimney of the fireplace was more or less intact, but Morgan said they would have to do without a fire. Even on a dark, rainy day smoke could be seen from far off. That could bring nosey neighbors asking questions. Worse than that, it could fetch some local lawman who would want to know what they were doing there. Morgan had an answer for that. They were on their way to Boise and had to find shelter from the cold and wet. But, as he explained, the less law they had to deal with, the better off they were.

They ate cold beans and biscuits, chewed on uncooked bacon. The driest place in the house was near the fireplace and that's where they slept. Before Morgan settled down he went outside and scanned the road with the binoculars. It was hard to see because of the rain and he gave up on it.

Propped up against the side of the fireplace, he thought it's past seven now and Uncle Bob is raising the roof or running to find the marshal. Morgan thought they were going to make it, but like the girl said, there were no guarantees. Morgan slept.

Three hours later they were back on the road, still tired and wet. Everybody cheered up when the rain stopped about two o'clock. The sun came out so hot, their clothes began to steam. They came to a town called McCall and were able to buy slickers and supplies in a store that sold everything. Morgan broke his own rule about not wasting time and they drank hot coffee and ate steak and eggs in a place at the end of town. Lord but the coffee tasted good, bad though it was.

One day followed another. It rained now and then, but mostly it was warm and sunny. Melanie, who had been drooping at the start of the long journey, was beginning to toughen up. She cooked all their meals—she didn't have to be much of a cook to fry bacon and beans—and the kid allowed as how every meal she prepared was delicious.

It took them six days to get to Boise. They could see the town when they topped a hill in the road about two miles out. Nightfall was still a few hours away and Morgan said they should wait until it was safe to go in.

The kid wanted to know where they were going to find the shawls and a hat with a veil for Melanie. Morgan said the slicker came down to her heels and she didn't need the shawls.

"Pull my hat down low over your eyes," he told her. When she did he backed away so he could see how it looked.

"Pull it down a little more," he said. "That's it. I think it'll do fine."

The kid said, "You're going to look funny without a hat. Everybody wears a hat."

"They'll just think I'm eccentric. I'll buy a new hat tomorrow morning."

Morgan timed it so it was full dark by the time they rode into Boise. He knew the Rathdrum Hotel, where the general was staying, because as a young man, half-drunk on beer, he had wandered in there and was promptly thrown out by three lumber camp foremen who were attending a Mormon convention. It wasn't his fault that he thought it might be a place where he could drink some more brew to round out the night.

Boise was a lot bigger these days. The railroad was there now and so were taller buildings. It had more banks, churches, whorehouses and saloons than in the wild old days when gold and silver were being taken out of the ground. Sporting citizens went boating on the Boise

River. There was a racetrack outside town and it was frowned on by the clergy.

Mercifully, thought Morgan, it was raining again. They rode in the rain and nobody gave them a second look. Three country-looking characters come to the big town to spend a few dollars.

One drunk did yell at Morgan, "Whyn't you buy yerself a hat, big fella. Nobody told you it's raining out?"

They passed the headquarters of the Idaho Party at Eighth and Hays. It occupied an entire commercial building and all four floors blazed with light. The Rathdrum Hotel was on Fifteenth Street. Morgan had no more than a dim memory of it, but knew that it was a temperance hotel that did most of its business with men who didn't drink, or men who used to drink too much but had given it up. When they got to it, Morgan thought it looked kind of grim. Inside, it smelled of religion, had the odor of good intentions.

Morgan had to knock hard on the general's door before Shandy Gibbons opened it. Gibbons wore his everyday clothes, but had a red nightcap perched on top of his bullet head. An Artillery Model Colt .45 was stuck inside the waistband of his pants and he had his right hand on the butt when he swung back the door.

"The general has retired for the night," he said, blocking the doorway with his bulk. "Whatever you want, it'll have to wait till morning. That's it. Come back in the morning. Don't you know the lateness of the hour?"

Morgan had to fight to control his temper. They had been on the road for six, rainy, lousy days; eating out of cans because it saved time; sleeping in wet clothes; and here was this ignorant Irish mick trying to give them a hard time of it.

"It's only nine-thirty, for Christ's sake. We have important information for the general. We must see him now."

Gibbons scowled at Morgan, ready to fight him. "And I'm telling you, mister, it'll have to wait. Come back tomorra with your information. That's my final word on it.''

Gibbons tried to close the door on them. That did it. Morgan slammed him in the face with the door and he staggered backwards, clawing at his face. Blood was coming from his nose.

"I'll murder you! I'll fucking murder you!'' he roared.

He was getting ready to make his rush when Gen. Howard came out of his bedroom wearing a worn dressing gown. His faded eyes blinked behind his reading glasses. He looked bewildered. ''What in the name of heaven is going on here? Gibbons, answer me.''

Gibbons looked ready to jump to attention, though he had been out of the army for years. ''A slight difference of opinion, sir. Morgan here wanted to talk to you. I said it was too late.''

"Nonsense!'' The general took off his reading glasses so he could see better. ''I was reading in my room.''

"Come in,'' he said to Morgan. ''Hello, Ticknor, back so soon. And who is this young lad?''

Melanie hadn't taken off Morgan's hat. Morgan snatched it off her head and the general said, ''Why it isn't a young lad a-tall. Good gracious!

Morgan said, ''This is Melanie Halliday, Drick Halliday's daughter.''

"Good Lord!!'' the general exclaimed. ''What does this mean?''

Morgan said, ''It means she wants to help us, help you in your work. There are things she wants to say at the meeting. Things about her father. I'd like to talk to you in private. Just a few moments, sir.''

The general looked at Melanie. ''Why can't the young lady speak for herself? I think that would be best. If it relates to her father, it's a very serious matter.''

Morgan and the kid were still standing there, not knowing what to do. Gibbons was holding a handkerchief to his damaged nose. The general waved his hand toward a chair and Melanie sat down.

Turning to Morgan and the kid, the general said, ''Why

don't you fellows go out and get yourselves something to eat. You must be hungry. The dining room here is closed now, but there are several reasonably priced restaurants in the neighborhood.''

The general looked at his great old lump of a silver watch. ''This young lady and I will have finished our talk by, say, ten-thirty. Get along with you now.''

Morgan and the kid went out.

Gibbons, who was by the door, hissed after them. ''You'll pay for what you done, Morgan. You and your sweetheart there.''

The kid spun around, his hand reaching for his gun. Morgan grabbed his hand before he could draw.

''Easy! Easy! He's just a stupid, ignorant mick. He does take good care of the general. That's all you can say for him.''

Morgan didn't turn the kid loose until he heard the bolt being shoved into place. Jesus Christ! Another second and Gibbons would be dead on the floor and the general would be without a bodyguard. Morgan didn't want the job. He had a ranch to run when this bullshit was out of the way.

They stood outside the hotel in the rain. It had tapered off to a drizzle, but it was still coming down. What the hell! They were as wet as they could get.

''What do you want to do?'' the kid asked. ''You want to eat?''

''Yes sir. I'm going to find the closest saloon and drink beer for an hour. And while I drink my beer I am going to dine on pigs' feet, sauerkraut, sour pickles, and other nourishing food.''

The kid was disgusted. ''Sounds like slop to me.''

Morgan said, ''You don't have to eat it. You can watch.''

Chapter Twelve

Morgan said they'd give the general more time than he'd asked for. It was a few minutes past eleven when they went back upstairs.

Morgan had been kidding about wanting to drink so much beer. Three beers could hardly be called a lot, even if they were schooners. The saloon had a short order cook and instead of the free lunch, Morgan got to eat scrambled eggs with ham, a double order of blueberry muffins.

The kid had the same and he ate in his usual ravenous way.

Gibbons opened the door and started up again with his whispered threats.

Morgan said, "Quit it or I'll tell the teacher and he'll make you wear a dunce cap. The other kids will laugh at you."

"Come on in, lads," the general called from an armchair by the fake fireplace. The Rathdrum hadn't always been a grim temperance hotel. Years back it had been kind of a swell place.

Melanie was in another armchair. "The general has been showing me some of his posters," she said to Morgan.

"Sit down. Sit down," the general said.

Morgan and the kid sat, waiting to hear how the talk came out.

Gen. Howard looked worn out and he rubbed the stump of his right arm before he spoke. "Miss Halliday will speak at our meeting next Sunday. At heart, I'm against the idea of having a daughter denounce her own father, no matter what he's done. Forgive me, Melanie."

Melanie spoke right up. "Please, sir, we've been over all that. I want to do it. If you change your mind I'll get a soapbox and a megaphone and shout my message on street corners."

Gen. Howard was alarmed at the prospect. "Goodness gracious! You can't do that. Those thugs will pelt you with rotten eggs, perhaps worse." Morgan noticed that he didn't called them Halliday's thugs.

"Then it's settled?" Melanie was firm.

The general sighed. "It's settled."

Morgan said, "We're latecomers here, sir. Where's this meeting to be held?"

"The old car barn on the corner of Ninth and Fort. The building takes up the entire block. It's a large building, but the city fathers want a newer, bigger one."

Morgan was surprised. "The mayor is letting you hold a meeting on city property?"

The general smiled. "No. The mayor wouldn't allow me to hold a meeting in the town dump. Last year the building was sold to a man named Joseph Hagerman, a builder, who has plans to tear it down and put something grander in its place. He's a wealthy man who can afford to defy the mayor and his cronies. Mr. Hagerman heard I was having trouble finding a place. He came to me and offered the use of his building. It's a great big old place and everything has been cleared out of it. Some of the old soldiers Shandy hired are guarding it now.''

Gibbons, hovering in the background, put his two cents in. "Most of them are not so old, General. A few are. But they're all good men and they're armed with Winchesters.''

The general held up his hand to stop Gibbons from making any more remarks. "All right, Shandy. I didn't mean to suggest that you had hired a bunch of old crocks.''

The general said, "The meeting is scheduled to begin at three o'clock. A good hour, I think. Allows the good people I hope to see there enough time to get back from church and eat their dinners.''

"What kind of a turnout do you expect?'' Morgan hoped it would be heavy.

"Well, I don't rightly know.'' The general had a notebook on the table beside him and he looked at it. "Perhaps I'm being optimistic, but I would say five-hundred, perhaps a little less than that. Many will come, I hope, out of curiosity. And I'm hoping to bring in some country people. They have more to lose if there's a war.''

"Doesn't sound so bad,'' Morgan said.

"The newspaper here—not Mr. Halliday's paper—has been giving me good coverage. They haven't printed any editorials supporting me, but give Howard a chance to be heard, is more their line. That's cautious, but fair enough.''

It was close to midnight and Morgan stood up. "Time we were going, sir. It's late.''

The general looked at his watch. "Not that late. Don't listen to Shandy. I'm not that tired.''

"But we are, sir.'' Morgan the diplomat.

The general walked with them to the door. Melanie

stayed where she was. "Miss Halliday will remain here. Shandy insists on sleeping on the sofa so he can watch the door." The sofa had a pillow at its head. The Greener 10-gauge lay on the floor beside it. "Miss Halliday can sleep in Shandy's room. Safer, don't you think?"

Morgan nodded. "Much safer." The 10-gauge, loaded with Double-0 buckshot, would stop anything that tried to get through that door.

"Come over in the morning and you can take a look at Mr. Hagerman's car barn. His workmen have done a good job on the old place and we've got flags up all over the walls. Some blackguards will be in the crowd, of course, but we hope to keep them under control."

Gibbons, still glowering on the sidelines, cut in with, "My men will deal with them." The general looked at him and he shut up.

"Goodnight, Morgan. Goodnight, Tick," Melanie called as they went out.

The general was too distracted to ask them where they were planning to get a room. Morgan was glad of that. It would be a bitch if he insisted that they put up at the Rathdrum. It was clean but grim, not an ounce of beer on the premises. There was a small hotel down the street, between the Rathdrum and the saloon they'd eaten in. Morgan had seen unescorted ladies going into it. That was the place for him, not that he planned to do any whoring this trip.

They went in and Morgan paid a week's rent for a room. He gave the kid some money. "That's for a dozen bottles of beer. I'm going up and lay down. You heard me tell the general how tired I am."

"Maybe we should go look at that car barn?" Like the general, the kid didn't approve of Morgan's beer drinking.

"You want to get shot, Tick? Gibbons's soldiers could take us for barn burners. It's still drizzling. Morning is time enough."

Morgan's Squaw

They had paid for a double room, but there was only one bed in it. It had a bathroom and Morgan took a quick dunk while the kid was getting the beer. He was under the covers, in his underpants, when the kid came back. Propped up by pillows, he uncapped a beer and drank from the bottle. The kid smelled a bit rank and Morgan told him to take a bath.

"I ain't sleeping with a billy goat," Morgan said firmly. "A bath, Tick."

Morgan drank another beer and pretended to be asleep when the kid came out of the bathroom. He didn't mind talking to a woman in bed, but he'd be damned if he'd lay there and converse with the kid like they were an old married couple. Something was wrong with that.

In a minute or two he didn't have to pretend. Beer and fatigue put him into a deep sleep that lasted all night. He woke up at five and lay in bed till five-thirty, then he shaved, put on his last clean shirt—still damp—and went down to the saloon for breakfast. It opened at six. He was back in the room by six-thirty. The kid didn't stir because he didn't sense danger.

Morgan let the kid sleep till eight. No use landing in on the general too early. He sat in an easy chair and read the Boise *Northwest Journal* from the day before. The paper gave the general and his meeting plenty of space. Boise was a small town in spite of its city airs. Not much happened there. So the general was news.

It was rumored, the news writer said, that the governor would attend the meeting as an impartial observer. Boise was the territorial capital and that would figure, Morgan thought. Maybe there wouldn't be any trouble if the governor came. He would have some armed guards with him.

Eastern newspaper reporters had been coming in by train. Scribblers from San Francisco, Chicago, Cleveland, St. Louis, Denver, would be in attendance. Good, Morgan thought.

Interviewed by the *Journal*, Drick Halliday was quoted as saying, "Let Howard have his circus, but when the speechifying is done with, and the smoke clears, the good people of Idaho will realize what a charlatan he is. I may attend the meeting and I may not. I have every right to be there, like any other citizen. Besides, I have received a personal invitation from the great man himself."

The *Journal* writer said Halliday seemed to regard the general and his cause as a joke. Something over-the-hill and out of date. Morgan thought he wouldn't find it such a joke when his daughter stood up there and told the crowd what a rotten, hypocritical bastard her father was. Morgan wondered what he would do. Walk out? Order his thugs to storm the platform? There would be a lot of broken heads if he did. Wait and see, nothing else for it.

He woke the kid.

Gen. Howard was waiting for them and they started out for the car barn. The general rode in the buckboard with Gibbons. Morgan, Melanie and the kid squeezed into a horse cab. Gibbon's ex-soldiers, toting Winchesters, were patrolling the front of the huge building when they got there. More of them were inside the building and out in back. Morgan thought they looked all right.

They saluted the general and the man in charge, a hard-faced youngish man with homemade sergeant's stripes sewn to the sleeve of his civilian coat, reported to Gibbons, who listened with the gravity of a senior officer.

"Quiet night, Mr. Gibbons," the man said. "Had some bother with kids, threw some rocks, nothing serious. Caught a man sneaking about. Thought he could be a spy. Turned out to be a drunk." Gibbons scowled and the man said quickly, "He was a drunk, sir. Puked in the gutter after we released him and lay there till the police carted him off."

Inside, the building was clean and empty, a great, echoing space. The enormous doors of the car barn were closed and they went in through a side door. A smell of axle grease still hung in the air. Wind blew through cracks in the building. At one end a speaker's platform had been set up. Gibbons's guards had been sitting or standing around. They stood to attention when the general came in.

"At ease, men," the general said.

Melanie got up on the platform and everybody looked at her. Back of the platform were doors like the ones in front. Morgan went to look at them and found them nailed shut with cross boards.

"Doors back there should be made to open," he told the general. "People should be able to get out if something happens. You don't want people trampled in a crush."

The general gave him a sharp look. "You're right. Gibbons, get those back doors opened up. Put a crossbar on them that can be easily removed. Put a man there, day and night."

Gibbons said, "Yes sir, rightaway," but he didn't like it. He glared at Morgan before he hurried away to relay the order to the hard-faced sergeant.

The general asked Morgan if he had any other suggestions.

Morgan couldn't think of any. The crowd would stand, no folding chairs. Good. Folding chairs could be used as weapons if a riot started.

"No, sir," he said. "It looks all right."

Gen. Howard, Melanie and Gibbons went back to the Rathdrum. Melanie had to squeeze in between the general and Gibbons, a tight fit because Gibbons was so thickbodied. Morgan said he and the kid were going to walk back.

"Mr. Hagerman is coming over at noon. Come by any time after that, if you feel like it." The general looked less tired today.

Morgan said they'd be along. In truth, he didn't feel like sitting around in a room with Gibbons in it. Or for that matter, sitting around any hotel room on such a nice day. The sun was out and the town was busy. They walked around, but finally they had to go back to their own room. Morgan bought a new shirt and pants, did the same for the kid. The kid wanted his new shirt and pants to be black. He wanted a black hat to go with the rest of his duds. Morgan bought it for him. When he put it on, he did look like a gunman. A Wild West show gunfighter. No real gunman ever dressed like that. Hickok looked like a riverboat gambler, John Wesley Hardin like the lawyer he was when he wasn't killing people.

Morgan didn't tell the kid.

That was Friday. They called on the general just to be polite, but didn't stay. Melanie wanted to go out. The general wouldn't allow it. "If you're bored, the bellboy will get you some ladies' magazines. Do you knit? I'm told it's very relaxing."

Melanie burst out laughing. "No, General, I don't knit."

Saturday was just as quiet. When they went to the general's rooms they found Melanie reading the paper, Gibbons leafing through ladies' magazines. The mick glared at them without saying anything. Melanie said the general was in his bedroom, working on his speech.

"You want me to tell him you're here?"

"Don't bother him. We're not staying long." Morgan thought he'd take a look-in at the saloon. Maybe he'd eat something. "You can stay," he said to the kid.

Melanie asked, "Why can't you stay?"

"I want to check on the horses," Morgan lied. The stable was a good one, no need to check on the horses.

Morgan sipped a beer in the saloon and chewed a ham sandwich. He was bored. Bored wasn't a word he used to

154

describe himself. It was more a lady's word. Just the same, he was bored.

He finished the beer and went back to the room. The kid came in soon after that.

"That Gibbons keeps looking at me. 'Somebody die in your family?' the fucker said. I guess the dark clothes. I had to get out of there before something bad happened. Melanie could have been hurt."

Nothing at all happened on Saturday.

On Sunday they went to the general's rooms hours before the meeting. This was the general's big day and Morgan wanted to be sure that nothing fucked it up. So far things had been quiet. No paid thugs yelling outside the hotel. No police protection had been provided for the general. Morgan hadn't seen a single bluecoat around.

They could kill the general on the way to the meeting. A sniper could do it from a window, a roof. Gibbons and all his guns wouldn't be much use then.

But the general wouldn't even consider riding in a closed cab. "Nonsense! You think they're going to kill me with all those reporters about?"

"Halliday may not care about reporters."

"I won't do it. That's the end of it. Say no more. I have more important things to think about."

Morgan wasn't ready to give up. "What if we get our horses and ride along beside you. Not like bodyguards, more like an escort."

The general glared at him. "More like utter nonsense, if you ask me. I'm telling you to drop it. That's an order, Sergeant Morgan."

At two o'clock they started out for the meeting place; the general up front in the buckboard, Melanie, Morgan and the kid following in a cab. It was a pleasant day, with a clear sky and a warm sun. Sunday afternoon, the streets were quiet.

Morgan watched the buildings on his side, the kid on

the other side. They had their rifles with them. Melanie was silent and tense. A woman from a store had come to the hotel to show her new dresses, new shoes. The dress she was wearing now was ladylike, but not fancy. An almost plain dress made of some soft, brown material. She wore ankle shoes with elastic sides. No hat. Her short straw-colored hair was bright with washing and brushed back like a boy's. Morgan thought she looked just fine. The kid found it hard to take his eyes off her.

They got there at 2:45. The big double doors hadn't been opened yet and Gibbons told the sergeant in charge to get it done. Along the front of the building, on both sides of the doors, trestle tables had been set up and women and girls were ladling out cups of lemonade and giving bottles of soft drinks to anybody who wanted them.

An old man with a cane called out, "Where's the free beer, Gineral?" when Howard got down from the buckboard.

"Try some lemonade," the general called back. "Better for you on a warm day."

That got a few laughs. There was a fair crowd waiting to get in. More people, many of them women, were coming from streets down from Ninth and Fort, where the building was. It looked like the general would get his four or five hundred after all. Morgan thought most everybody he saw there had the same look, a mixture of jokiness and don't-try-to-fool-me. But there was real curiosity. The women were open about it. The men tried to hide it.

When Melanie got out of the cab, a murmur ran through the crowd like a hot wind. Those who recognized her, mostly women, gobbled like turkeys. Those who didn't know her soon got an earful. She carried a red leather pocket Bible that Morgan had seen in the General's sitting room and that caused as much whispering and gobbling as Melanie herself. Morgan wondered what she was doing with a Bible.

The crowd was drifting in now. Morgan went ahead of them to make sure the back doors had been seen to. He knew Gibbons had told the sergeant in charge. That didn't mean that it had been done. Orders had a way of getting lost.

The cross boards that nailed the door shut had been removed. A crossbar and two side slots had been installed. Morgan lifted the crossbar to make sure it wasn't too tight a fit. It was all right. But he lifted the bar out of the slots and pushed the doors open, so nothing would be left to chance. There was nobody in the street.

Like all meetings, this one didn't start on time. It was ten past three and more and more people were coming in. Morgan figured there had to be more than 500 by now. Maybe it was closer to six. Too many people even for such a large space. It was getting hot in the barn, so many bodies packed together. He thought of opening the rear doors and decided against it. The platform was too close to the rear doors. Anybody standing there, or in the street, would have a clear shot at the general's back.

On the platform were six folding chairs. Melanie, Gibbons and a man that Morgan took to be Joseph Hagerman sat on three of them. The general was at the lectern, fiddling with his notes. Two ex-soldiers, without their Winchesters, stood at either end of the platform. Their pistols were stuck in their belts and covered by their coats. Morgan and the kid stood behind the ones on the right. From there they could watch the crowd.

The general cleared his throat and was about to begin when there was a commotion in the back of the crowd. At first Morgan thought the governor had arrived, then he saw Halliday coming through the crowd which parted for him like the Red Sea. Neal, the editor, and another man were dogging along behind him. No thug bodyguards. Morgan figured they were outside.

Halliday's face had storm warnings in it. It was darker

than Morgan remembered it. The fucker didn't look like a half-Indian, but there was Indian in him. He had his anger under control. Just barely. Somebody had run and told him about the daughter. He kept coming until he was right in front of the platform.

For a moment Morgan thought he was about to jump up on the platform and drag his daughter out of there. The crowd was enjoying this. What a melodrama! But all Halliday did was stand there with his arms folded. He didn't look at his daughter, sitting demurely, holding the Bible in her lap. Morgan thought Halliday was staring, but not seeing anything. Neal, to one side of him, looked nervous. The other man, portly and stolid, just stood there, holding the lapels of his frock coat with both hands.

Gen. Howard began to speak. Fluent enough in private conversation, he was not a good public speaker. His voice was reedy and it didn't carry far. One by one, he made his points, sometimes referring to his notes. At one point a man shouted from the back, "Louder, Gineral. We can't hear you back here." He sounded like the old boozer with the cane.

Gen. Howard tried to raise his voice without much success. He plodded on, reminding his listeners of how bad the war of '77 had been. He said the Nez Perce went to war only when they were threatened with the loss of their lands, theirs by treaty right. That got some booing, but it wasn't too bad. They let him continue. He said the war of '77 was a thing of the past. The question was, ten years later, in this year of 1887, did they want another Indian war? Looking directly down at Halliday, he launched an attack on Halliday's "Godless ideas," his "un-Christian" hatred of the Indians, his "reckless ambition," all of which were threatening to plunge the territory into a savage, bloody war. Once started, he said, such a war would not be quickly or easily ended.

Still looking down at Halliday, he begged him to look

into his heart and try to find the goodness that must have been there in his youth, was surely still there, if only he'd try to find it again. He urged Halliday to get up on the platform and admit he was wrong.

"I will pray with you and for you," the general said.

Halliday didn't move a muscle.

Gen. Howard took a drink of water and a wave of his hand brought Melanie to the lectern. She still clutched the Bible and her face was defiant. Her father's face had no expression at all, but Morgan could feel the black hatred in the man. He wouldn't have been surprised if Halliday had tried to pull a gun, tried to shoot her dead, crowd or no crowd. Morgan was waiting for that. So was the kid. Halliday didn't even move.

Melanie had a good, strong voice, a stagy sense of her ability to sway a crowd. "My name is Melanie Halliday and I am the daughter of that man standing there, Drick Halliday, my father." The crowd remained dead silent. "I am going to tell you about my father, the kind of man he is." Melanie held up the Bible, then she kissed it. "I swear by this Bible and Almighty God and on the grave of my dead mother—my murdered mother—that every terrible thing I am about to tell you is true."

Melanie paused to let that sink in.

The crowd gasped and muttered and shifted its feet and several women shouted, "Shame! Shame! You lie! You're a liar! Get down from there before God strikes you dead!" Others wanted to listen, and they were in the majority. There was some pushing and shoving, some hitting and name calling, before the crowd settled down.

Melanie took a deep breath. "There he stands, the man who killed my mother, the man who punched her in the stomach once too often. He always struck her in the body. He was afraid to hit her in the face because the marks would show. My mother was in great pain after that last and final beating. But my hypocrite of a father refused to

159

send for a doctor until she was safely dead. And do you know what the doctor put on the death certificate? *Heart failure*!'' Melanie shouted the words until her voice cracked

She continued in a quieter voice that still carried to the back of the crowd. ''The doctor didn't even examine her body. Why should he, after all? The mighty Drick Halliday had spoken, and who was he to doubt his word? So she was buried and forgotten. She had a fine funeral, as you may remember, but it was more a display of my father's wealth than any respect for my mother.''

Melanie paused, but the crowd remained silent. Halliday still hadn't moved. Nothing his daughter said registered in his dark, handsome face. Morgan couldn't imagine what he was thinking. Neal's thin face was white, as if the accusations had been leveled at him.

Melanie lowered her voice even more but it still carried. ''I have carried this terrible secret with me since my mother's death. Why you ask, did I not speak up before this? The simple truth is I was afraid. Terrified of my own father. My father threatened to put me in an asylum for the insane if I told anyone what he had done. Instead— because of the disgrace it would bring—he sent me to his trading post in Grangeville, where I was kept a prisoner by his brother Robert, a drunken savage who whipped me when I locked my bedroom door against him.''

Well now, Morgan thought, she's starting to add a little spice here. He'd seen nothing to indicate that Uncle Bob was a drunkard or a savage. His brother had foisted his daughter on him and he was trying to make the best of it. Sure he was cranky, but that was about the size of it.

Melanie went on. ''My Uncle Robert is of no importance. All he does is run a trading post. On the other hand, my father is a man of great ambition. He would be the king, the emperor of Idaho, if you let him. His plan to remove the Indians is a sham and a fraud. There is no

Indian menace. The only menace is him. Some of the filthy wretches who work for him have been dressing up as Indians and attacking white ranchers and farmers. My father's agents have been paying them well to kill and burn. A fantastic accusation, you think? Far from it, I heard him talking about it to some men long before it started. My mother was alive then and I had no interest in my father's activities. But I remember the conversation he had with those men. And now what he suggested to them is happening. The Indian war he wants so badly is not far off. And what will happen to your homes and families? My father doesn't give a damn about you. Why should he? The Savior of Idaho can't be bothered with such petty concerns. Listen to Gen. Howard. I would not have had the courage to come here if not for him. Listen to the general. Don't listen to my father. He is an evil, wicked man.''

Suddenly, Melanie seemed to lose control. She left the lectern and walked to the edge of the platform where she stared down at her father. She still held the Bible in one hand. Both hands were shaking.

"Damn you! Damn! Damn! Damn you! Why don't you get up here and deny everything I've said. Deny that you beat me and raped me when my mother was sick and you didn't want her. What kind of man would rape a little girl of thirteen? Your own daughter! Your own daughter! I hate you! May you burn in hell!!'' She screamed a despairing scream and flung the Bible at him. It struck him in the face and fell to the floor.

Still with no expression on his face, Halliday turned and walked out, followed by his cronies.

Up on the platform, Melanie was crying. Gen. Howard had his arm around her, trying to comfort her.

The crowd gaped at the scene in silence.

Chapter Thirteen

Melanie was back in her chair, drinking a glass of water and still crying. Gibbons was saying something to her. She kept shaking her head. Joseph Hagerman offered her his handkerchief and she took it and dabbed at her eyes. Gen. Howard was back behind the lectern. A man picked up the Bible and put it on the edge of the platform. The crowd was restless, but didn't want to leave. Melanie had given them a great show and Lord knows what else she'd do.

"My friends," the general said. "You have heard some shocking things today. I am as shocked as you are. But we must leave Cedric Halliday's private sins to his Maker. Let he who is without sin cast the first stone. God is good. God is forgiving and for even a sinner such as Cedric Halliday there is always hope if he repents."

Fuck you, General, Morgan thought. Melanie put on a great, lying performance and you're trying to take the bite out of it. But maybe a lot of good people won't buy your God-is-good bullshit.

Morgan's Squaw

"I ask you to pray for Cedric Halliday," the general was saying. "At the same time, I must ask you to reject him as a leader for he is not fit to lead. He has lied to you, has endangered your lives and those of your families with his demagoguery, his rabble-rousing, his demented hatred of the Indians. Reject him. Do not listen to him. His day is done."

Drick Halliday had been gone for ten minutes and the general was still at it. He was beginning to repeat himself. Melanie had stopped crying and was whispering something to Joseph Hagerman. The show was over and some of the people in back were edging out the door. Some in front, and in the middle, were finding it hard to get out. But even after maybe 50 people left, a tight jam of bodies remained.

Morgan was wishing the general would wrap it when somebody yelled, "Fire!" A woman screamed, then another, and the crowd started to panic. The side of the building was on fire and the old dry wooden building started to go up. Everybody was trying to get to the open doors. Women were screaming. Men were shouting. In the surge toward the doors people went down and were getting trampled. Morgan cupped his hands and shouted, "You can get out the back way. I'll open the door."

Flames were shooting up the side wall and the roof was catching fire. Morgan got to the door and found the guard trying to open it. The crossbar had been thrown to one side. Morgan and the guard put their shoulders to the door, but it wouldn't budge.

"Save yourself," Morgan said to the guard. He ran back to the platform. Melanie was still there, staring up at the burning roof. She was biting her knuckles and moving her mouth without making a sound. Joseph Hagerman was gone, lost somewhere in the panicked, shoving, screaming crowd. The kid had been knocked down by people rushing the wrong way. He struggled to his feet and got up on the platform.

"Get her out of here," Morgan yelled, pointing at Melanie. The kid grabbed her, but she struggled with him. The roof above the platform was burning fiercely, close to collapse. Melanie shoved the kid away and covered her face with her hand. A chunk of burning wood fell from the roof and struck her on the head. She went down with blood all over her. The roof was high and the chunk of wood had fallen a long way. Morgan could see where it had caved in the top of her skull. He felt her heart. It was still beating. He knew she'd die, but he told the kid to carry her out of there.

About half the crowd had shoved their way out. Those jammed together too far to the front were still struggling and screaming. Bodies lay unconscious or dead on the door. Flaming boards were still dropping down from the roof. It hadn't collapsed yet. A firebell sounded, then another. Morgan heard men shouting outside the back door. Then the door opened and firemen ran in shouting, "Out this way! Out this way!"

The people still up front started rushing for the back. More bodies went down. Not all of them got up. People were climbing over the platform. It collapsed under their weight. Morgan saw the general fall off the stage, his clothes on fire. Gibbons fought his way to him, slung him over his shoulder, and carried him out. The kid lifted Melanie and carried her out in his arms.

Morgan got out just in time. The roof came down with a thunderous crash. One fireman said to another, "It's a goner. Just as well let it burn itself out."

Morgan grabbed one of the firemen by the arm. The fireman tried to pull himself loose. Morgan tightened his grip. "What was wrong with the door? I couldn't get it open."

"It was jammed shut with a wagon. Over there." The fireman pointed. "It's loaded with rocks. It took four of us to move it."

Morgan let go of the fireman's arm and went over to

where Gen. Howard sat on the sidewalk with his back against the wall. Both his hands were in a fire bucket filled with water. Gibbons was hunkered down beside him, dabbing at his face with a water soaked handkerchief.

Morgan hunkered down too. "How is he?"

"Bad enough. He's an old man." Gibbons squeezed out the handkerchief and soaked it again.

Morgan stood up. "Where are the kid and the girl?"

Gibbons stared up at him. "I don't know and I don't care. Are there any ambulances coming, for Christ's sake. Go and take a look. Got to get the general to a hospital."

Three ambulances were pulled up in front of the building. One of them was only half full of injured people, but the driver was getting ready to take off. Morgan yelled at him to stop. The driver was saying he had to get these injured people to the hospital when Gibbons came around the corner, carrying the general over his shoulder.

"Put him in the next ambulance," the driver shouted. "I got a full load."

Gibbons drew a pistol with his free hand and told the driver he'd shoot him dead if he moved the ambulance. Then he lifted the general into the ambulance and got in after him. The doors were closed and the ambulance rolled away.

Morgan got hold of an ambulance man, an older man, with some kind of stripes on his sleeve. "You see a kid dressed all in black carrying an injured girl over his shoulder?"

"Ambulance already took them away. Girl looked dead to me. Sorry if she's your kin."

The man told Morgan how to get to the hospital. He got there in five minutes in a cab. The emergency room was crowded with injured people, people with severe burns. Some were clamoring for attention. Some were slumped in silence. Gen. Howard wasn't there.

A harried looking nurse tried to dodge around Morgan when he barred her way. He got in front of her again, asked the same question about the kid and the girl.

"The girl was dead when they brought her in. She's in the morgue." The nurse pushed past Morgan and stepped over an unconscious man lying on the floor. It was the old boozer with the cane and he was drunk, or badly injured, or both.

Morgan went out to the reception desk to ask about the general. The kid was there, slumped in a chair.

"I was waiting for you," he said in a toneless voice. "Melanie's dead. Died on the way here. Anyway, she's dead."

"I know." The kid was taking it hard. Morgan didn't say anything more about the girl. "Where's the general?"

"In a room, I guess. I don't know where he is."

"Come on. Let's try to find him."

The nurse at the desk looked in a book and said Gen. Howard was in Room 37. "But you can't go up there right now. The doctor is with him. You'll have to wait."

"Is his driver with him? A big Irishman."

"That's different. The general asked that he be allowed to go up."

Morgan said, "Then why can't we be allowed? I'm his son and this is his grandson. I'm Morgan. He's Tick."

The nurse gave him a thin-lipped smile. "I don't think I believe you. But whoever you are, you'll have to wait. I'll check and let you know."

Morgan and the kid sat down on a bench. The kid didn't say anything for a while. "It was Halliday's badmen that started that fire."

"Yes, they did."

"I'm going to do something about it."

"I think that's a good idea. I'll go with you. But first I want to see the general, find out how he is."

"I don't want to wait too long. If they make us wait too long, I'm leaving."

They didn't.

Morgan's Squaw

Morgan and Tick rushed up to Room 37 but it looked as if the old man wouldn't be doing any talking for a while. No sense wasting time here. They might as well get on with what had to be done.

"Where are you going?" Gibbons asked as Morgan turned toward the door.

"What's it to you?" Morgan had first delayed what had to be done, because he wanted to have a few words with the general but it was pointless now.

Gibbons said, "You have the look of a man that's going to do something drastic. You're going after Halliday. Isn't that right?"

Morgan nodded. "That's right."

Gibbons got up from the chair. "I'll come with you. Me and the 10-gauge, the heavy artillery, so to speak. After what his daughter said, the fire, I'd say Halliday's ship is listing bad by now. But not all the rats will desert the sinking ship. He'll manage to hang on to a few. They'll be the real hard cases. You're going to need me and the 10-gauge."

"Come if you're coming." Morgan didn't want to hear any more about what he needed. He needed more than he had. He needed Wyatt and Doc.

Downstairs, the buckboard was hitched right in front of the hospital. Gibbons felt under the cushions to make sure the Sharps was there. "I'm thinking the general will be all right till I get back."

If you get back, Morgan thought.

They got up on the box and it was a good thing the kid was skinny. Gibbons picked up the reins. "I'm thinking the word on Halliday will be all over by now. The way his daughter screamed at him at the end, you could tell it was the gospel truth. What girl could make up such awful things and shout them in public?"

Melanie could, Morgan thought.

"He's a ruined man, that Halliday. Ruined and disgraced."

Morgan told Gibbons to hitch the horse two blocks down from the Idaho Party clubhouse. It was getting on toward evening and the street would have been quiet except for the military march music blaring from the direction of the clubhouse. The noisy brass band music had to be coming from there. This was a commercial section and all the businesses were closed. There wasn't a sign of a headbeater or a bluecoat.

The music got louder as they got closer. Other noises came from the open windows of the second floor. Men were whooping and laughing and stomping their feet on a wooden floor.

Gibbons gestured with the unwrapped shotgun. It was a heavy weapon and would have looked ungainly in smaller hands. "What has Halliday got to celebrate about?" Gibbons said bitterly. "His daughter dead and the general as good as."

"I doubt if he's celebrating," Morgan said.

Most of the windows of the clubhouse building had been broken and shards of glass lay on the sidewalk. A huge picture of Halliday, with a man-of-destiny look, had been smeared by rotten eggs. Halliday's star was taking a real fall.

The downstairs door was unlocked and unguarded and Morgan wondered if Halliday figured they'd be along. They would just have to go upstairs and find out. The music was enough to wake the dead and that in itself was peculiar. It could be that Halliday wasn't there at all, just what was left of his hard cases drinking the free whiskey, having themselves one last wild party before the money stopped.

Morgan listened as best he could. No women's voices that he could hear. It wouldn't be so good if women were up there. They went up the stairs and no hidden shooters started blasting. The military music blared on. It had to be coming from an Edisonphone machine with the big horn. He didn't know much about it. Sounds, the human voice, music, anything, were recorded on wax disks, something like that, and could be played on the machine. Politicians all over were using the noisemaker to add beef.

He didn't know what was on the second floor, but the way the music echoed, it had to be a large space like a meeting room. They got to the door and it was half open. It was a meeting room, a big one, and there was the smell of new wood and varnish. Whoever was in there had to be at the far end of the room and he couldn't see them. They could be in cover, waiting for the door to open all the way.

Gibbons went in first because he had the big shotgun. Morgan and the kid followed him and nobody saw them at first. Halliday sat behind a desk with a bottle and glass in front of him. Neal sat to one side of him, looking drunk and bewildered. Six hard cases, not headbeaters but real gunmen, were dancing around the fat man Morgan had seen at the general's meeting. They kept turning the fat man this way and that. His face was red with whiskey and anger.

Halliday spotted them and jumped to his feet with a roar louder than the music machine. "Morgan! Morgan! You finally came and you brought friends! You know what you did today, you son-of-a-bitch!"

The fat man broke away from his tormenters and shut off the machine. It was dead quiet for a few seconds and he tried to say something. Another roar from Halliday left him silent and shaking.

Halliday came out from behind the desk. Morgan had expected him to try to duck for cover, but he was too drunk or angry to do the smart thing. Halliday wore a short-barreled Sheriff's Model Colt .45 on a plain brown belt. Some of the gunmen carried two guns, one holstered, one stuck in their waistbands. No rifles or shotguns were in sight.

"You started it," Morgan said quietly. "This is going to end here."

"Not yet!" Halliday shouted. "You brought my daughter here to throw her filthy lies in my face. I never killed her mother. I never raped her. I threatened her with the madhouse because she's crazy. I sent her to my brother to keep her out of the way. My brother finally got word to me that you'd taken her, you spying sneak. You disgraced a movement that would have changed this territory into the finest state in the Union."

Halliday looked like he was ready to make his move. He didn't. Morgan didn't think it was because of the 10-gauge. Halliday was drunk and shouting mad and the big shotgun didn't bother him.

All his anger was directed at Morgan. "Who are you? What are you? A stinking two-bit horse trader! Where do you get the nerve to take on a man like me? You kidnapped my daughter and dragged her all the way here to throw dirt on my good name, the crazy bitch!!"

Gibbons had the shotgun pointed at the six gunmen and it was making them nervous. Halliday was shouting again when one of the gunmen pulled a gun and fired two fast shots at Gibbons and missed. The 10-gauge boomed and four gunmen went down in a welter of blood. Halliday went for his gun and Morgan shot him twice in the chest and he dropped. One of the two gunmen left killed Gibbons with a head shot and he hit the floor. Morgan killed the gunman who fired the shot. The kid killed the last gunman as he tried to make a run for the door.

The fat man had his hands up and was begging for mercy. Morgan told him to get down on the floor and stretch his hands out in front of him. The fat man got down on the floor and shit his pants. The kid was running for the desk to get at Neal, blubbering behind it. He was raising his gun, taking aim.

"Don't kill him," Morgan shouted. "Put up the gun

or I'll shoot your arm off. We need the fucker.''

The kid turned with the gun in his hand, then his shoulders slumped as he dragged Neal out from behind the desk. Neal was close to collapse. At least he didn't dirty his pants, Morgan thought. The kid back-handed Neal across the face and Morgan told him to quit it. But it was understandable. He wanted to do much worse.

"Search him for a derringer," Morgan said. "Watch him good."

The meeting hall reeked of gunsmoke, shit and blood. The kid was going through Neal's pockets, tossing their contents onto the desk. Morgan kept listening for police wagon bells. There were none.

He walked over to the fat man and put his pistol to the back of his head. "Straight answers now or I'll blow your brains out. What's your name and what did you do for Halliday?"

"Edward Tazewell. I was his Boise accountant, other places."

"Then you know how his money was spent?"

The fat man wasn't through shitting and the stench got worse. Morgan had to cock the .45 to get an answer.

"Yes, that's right. I have the books, but I had nothing to do with what he was doing. I sent money to Neal over there, other people. I'll tell you anything you want to know."

"Will you testify in court?"

"Just don't kill me. I'll testify to anything."

Morgan holstered his gun and kicked the fat man in the side. "Just don't change your mind or I'll be waiting for you. Now get up, you crooked bastard, and don't say another word."

Morgan turned to the kid. "We're taking these fuckers to police headquarters. Chief may not be glad to see us, but he'll see us. Halliday had him bribed or threatened. No matter. That fire killed a lot of people. He'll want to come out of this as clean as he can. Come on now. Let's get moving."

They left Gibbons with the other dead men and went downstairs with the prisoners. Three hours later they were back at the hospital. On the way there the kid said he'd like to come back to Spade Bit.

"Melanie getting killed has took the heart out of me. Her father was lying about her, wasn't he?"

"Sure he was." Morgan wasn't sure at all. But it didn't matter now.

If she had lied, her lies had destroyed her father and his Indian-hating movement, and they would go to the grave with both of them. The fat accountant has signed a statement implicating Neal, and the chief of police, an oily bastard, was certain he could work on Neal and make him confess.

The kid said, "What about me coming back to Spade Bit. After what we've been through, hard work looks good."

Morgan cringed at the idea. "I have a better idea. How about you take over as the general's driver? He's going to need somebody."

"Me!" The kid was startled, then he sort of liked the idea. "You think he'd have me?"

"Why not? You helped him stop Halliday and he can't forget that. And I'll add my two cents, which ought to be worth something. Think of all the places you'll get to go. Washington, D.C., New York, so on. All the pretty girls you'll get to meet."

They were getting close to the hospital. The kid stopped and said, "You don't want me at Spade Bit?"

" 'Fraid I don't. You're not cut out for the life there. With the general you'll be doing something you'll come to like, which is protecting a good man. What do you say."

"Golly," the kid said.

Inside the hospital, at the registration desk, the nurse called out, "Favorable news. Gen. Howard is conscious and has been asking for you."

Morgan and the kid started for the stairs. "Let's go up and work on him."